THE
Forbidden
BOOK

LQ

LEVINE QUERIDO

MONTCLAIR · AMSTERDAM · HOBOKEN

This is an Arthur A. Levine book
Published by Levine Querido

LQ

LEVINE QUERIDO

www.levinequerido.com • info@levinequerido.com

Levine Querido is distributed by Chronicle Books, LLC

Library of Congress Control Number: 2023951872
ISBN 978-1-64614-456-3

Printed and bound in China

Published in October 2024
First Printing

Pip—this one is for you.

CHAPTER

1

ON A FULL MOON NIGHT, after a day of fasting, the young bride Sorel Kalmans leapt from a window and left her life behind.

All day, Sorel had been pacing up and down her room like a caged fox, a feeling building inside her that she could not ignore. She could not marry. She would not marry. The girl who was supposed to walk to the wedding canopy, to walk seven circles around the son of her city's rebbe—she could not imagine herself as that girl. Her hands were not that girl's hands, which her nursemaid had scrubbed free of dirt and bathed in milk for a week to soften. When she looked at herself dressed in the heavy embroidered skirts of her wedding dress, her red hair pinned up and braided and threaded with gold, she saw a stranger. The modern cut of the dress, with its nipped waist, gave her body an alien shape. Her own feet, too light in delicate slippers, kept tripping her.

You have to leave, the stranger told her from the shadowy reflection of her polished silver mirror. She might have found the face pretty, had she not been trying to see it as her own, and beneath the plucked brows and lip and the delicate brush of powder over her freckles, she couldn't find any trace of herself.

"How can I leave?" Sorel asked. "Kalman Senderovich's daughter, who's supposed to marry the Esroger Rebbe's oldest son and heir. Where would I go? Everyone would be looking for me."

Some things, said the girl in the mirror, *are simply unbearable. It does not matter where you go or what you do, as long as you do not let this happen.*

And then another voice, as clear as if someone were standing directly behind her. The sound of it made her turn, startled, to find the room empty.

If you can't run alone, the voice had said, *I'll take you.*

It was dizziness. The fasting, and the pacing, and the heat in her room—she felt the room was stifling, for a spring night. She was as good as dreaming; she'd heard nothing.

But she said, "Please."

And with her next breath, she felt herself changing. The trapped fox had seen that the trap was only a loop of rope, so simple to undo. There was the window, and there, across the cluttered stable-yard, was the gate that led to the road and the river and the woods.

Her maid was waiting in the hall, with strict orders not to let Sorel cause a scene—her father had already seen the glint of madness in her eyes and locked her in her room to stop it from showing until it was too late. But she didn't need to use the door. She suddenly could not remember how it felt to be afraid of the jump.

In a single motion, she ran to the window, threw open the sash, and leapt.

FOR HALF A BREATH, Sorel thought she might never land. That she was flying, or that the earth would open up and swallow her. Then some instinct made her twist herself sideways, and she landed on her left hip in the mud, gasping at the pain of impact on her wrist. She crawled a few steps and hauled herself up by the wheel of a carriage, one of several the rebbe's disciples had left scattered around the yard.

Earlier, she remembered, she had seen the gentile stable-boy go into the house, joining the other servants for their portion of tonight's feast—everyone but Sorel herself would be celebrating. The boy slept in one of the stalls; he would be wearing his Sunday clothes for the feast, but he kept the clothes he wasn't wearing wrapped in a bundle in the rafters.

Energized by the unfolding of a plan, Sorel slipped between the carriages and into the stable. There was the boy's coat, wrapped around his spare shirt and trousers. She tucked it under her arm without stopping to unwrap it. A long knife hung from a nail beside the bundle, and her hand reached for it before she could give it any thought. She knew it was a prized possession, clean and polished, its leather sheath lovingly decorated with a motif of flowers. But it would be foolish to go anywhere without a knife, so she took it.

No one had yet raised an alarm as she left the stable-yard, turning not right toward town but left, toward the forest. There was a little footbridge, and there she paused to strip out of her gown, already heavy on its own but now dragging her backward at every step, its hem clumped with mud. After cutting through the bodice with the stable-boy's knife, she stepped out of the gown, balled it up, and threw it in the water.

A dog barked somewhere in the darkness, and then she heard a man cry an alarm. Without waiting to see the dress sink, she slipped into the trees, shoving her way through the underbrush as the clamor of voices rose and spread behind her.

The brambles caught at her hair. She reached up, yanked out the hairpins, and tucked them into her stocking. She chopped wildly at her braids until they fell from her shoulders, and freed from the trap, she leapt forward, not caring what direction she ran.

SOREL WAS THOROUGHLY LOST by the time she stopped, panting and shivering, to unwrap her stolen bundle of clothes. The stable-boy was shorter than herself, but broader, so she belted the trousers with a stocking, tucking her hairpins into the pocket. There, they jingled faintly, a comforting weight. She could at least trade them for a meal, she thought, a little practical worry catching up as she noticed that her embroidered slippers were pinching her feet, her chest ached, and her wrist was twinging from the way she'd landed in the stable-yard.

"All worth it," she told herself out loud. She wrapped the stable-boy's coat around herself and took a deep breath, smelling horse and forest and mud. Her feet were cold, but now, dressed in wool, the rest of her was warm enough. She no longer heard the voices of her pursuers: she might have lost herself, but she'd lost them, too. She heard only the soft scuttling of little night animals and the creaking of branches in the slight breeze overhead. After a moment a dog barked, far away, and quieted again.

She did not feel alone. She had herself, and she had the knife, which felt good in her hand and hung with reassuring weight at her hip when she looped its cord around her stocking belt. Without the weight of her hair, her head felt lighter and she could stand with her shoulders back, proud. Even the aches and pains came to her with a sense of curiosity, as if she were learning the feel of someone else's limbs, the numbness of panic wearing off.

She started walking, slower now, savoring the texture of the ground below her feet, trying to stay on a straight path by keeping the moon to one side. When the sun rose, she would know her directions, and she could make her way to Esrog. The city was big enough that surely she could find a way to disappear, to become someone else.

She felt capable almost of walking all the way to Krakow or Odessa or Paris.

THE CITY OF ESROG sat within the gentle curve of a river. Kalman Senderovich, the lumber merchant, sent his wares to the sea down that same river, from the shtetl he ruled over miles upstream. Between the shtetl and city was the tangle of forest in which Sorel had lost herself, walking until her eyelids drooped and the ache in her feet became overwhelming. At some time during the night she'd come upon a stone wall, tucked herself into its shadow, and fallen asleep curled up beneath her woolen coat.

She woke to the sound of a woman's voice singing. The spot where she was sleeping lay low down, not far from the river, and the sound carried oddly in the morning fog. Sorel sat up slowly, wrapping herself again in the coat. The voice was a clear, low alto, unexpectedly beautiful, singing a folk song in Yiddish from the other side of the wall.

When Sorel got to her feet, she saw that her resting place was just outside the boundary of a cemetery. The stone wall, moss-eaten, barely kept the trees back from the cluster of gravestones, their weathered faces whispering names in Hebrew letters.

The singing woman was walking between the jumbled lines of headstones with a rag in her hand, brushing dead leaves and dried mud from their surfaces as she sang to herself. A couple of crows hopped after her, searching for grubs in the earth that she'd disturbed. She was old, stooped, her voice stronger than her frail appearance, and dressed in rags. Sorel must have made some noise, because the old woman stopped singing and turned, but tilting her ear rather than looking: she must be blind.

"Is there someone there?" she asked. The crows, at her feet, echoed her with a harsh "rekh, rekh."

Sorel opened her mouth to speak, coughed, and said hoarsely, "Good morning."

The old woman laughed. "Are you a ghost, or a living boy? Let me feel your hand."

She reached out, and Sorel went to her.

"A living boy," she said, pleased with how it felt, and shook the woman's rough, dry hand.

"Are you on your way to the wedding feast?" the old woman asked. "I was on my way, but I always stop by the cemetery first, to bring the news to the dead, whenever something happens."

A klogerin—a cemetery caretaker. Sorel wondered if this was the same old woman who sometimes haunted the cemetery back home, where her mother was buried.

"Wedding feast?" she asked, and, grasping for a story, "I'm not from here, I'm traveling. Only slept here because I was lost in the dark."

"The rebbe's son is getting married," the old woman explained. "The Esroger Rebbe—you'll have heard of him, surely! They must know him all the way to the Holy Land. The rebbe has invited a hundred beggars to a feast at the Great Synagogue, in honor of the occasion."

Sorel felt herself smiling. Why not? She thought. Why not attend her own wedding feast? Her stomach was griping at her anyway. Would anyone look for her among a crowd of beggars at the Great Synagogue in Esrog?

"Like I said, I'm lost," she said.

"I'll show you, if you'll give me your arm," the old woman said, taking it without waiting for an answer. She had seemed perfectly capable on her own, but she leaned her weight on Sorel with a sigh of relief, so it must have been taking her more effort to walk the rough ground than it had appeared.

The little cemetery was tucked among the trees, a root heaving the stones of the wall aside here and there, and the path back to the road scarcely visible. Keeping her eyes down to help the old woman place her feet and to avoid pebbles on her own bare soles, Sorel felt a chill at the sight of large pawprints crossing their path. They were nearly half the length of her feet, belonging either to a massive dog or a wolf. Had someone brought dogs to look for her? She would surely have heard them. It must have been a wild animal, and soon enough she'd be inside the city wall and sleeping among people, instead of on bare earth.

"What is your name, tatele?" said the klogerin, interrupting Sorel's thoughts.

"Israel," she said, grasping for a name that sounded familiar. "Isser . . . Jacobs."

"They call me Rukhele," the old woman said and patted Sorel's arm. "Don't you worry. All the beggars and thieves in Esrog know Old Rukhele, and no one will bother you while you're with me."

It hadn't occurred to Sorel to worry about beggars and thieves. She'd been thinking about lumbermen, the gentiles her father hired, or the rebbe's disciples. "Thank you, Rukhele. I do also have a knife."

Rukhele patted her arm again, as if Sorel were a student who'd made an astute observation. They picked their way along the path until the underbrush opened up and Sorel saw on one side the river, and on the other side the dust and mud of the road, churned up by horses' hooves and cut deeply by wheel ruts. Rukhele had not exaggerated about the wedding feast, for little knots of people clad in rags were making their way along it, and Rukhele, hearing a voice she must have known, steered Sorel toward one of these groups. It was a group of old women, clearly old friends, and they had soon slipped into a conversation she didn't understand, Rukhele releasing Sorel's arm to lean instead on one of her companions. She was glad that she could see the city ahead—she didn't think she could stand to walk much farther. She could scarcely walk any faster than bent little Rukhele, though Sorel's legs were much longer.

Her mind wandered until she felt a prickle in the back of her neck, as if someone were watching her. When she turned, there was a young man a few paces behind—better dressed than the beggars, but with the worn shoes and bulky pack of a peddler. He had been staring at Sorel's back with intensity, but when she caught his eye, he smiled at her. There was nothing wrong with the smile, but she didn't trust it. It looked a little bit like the smile a boy might give a girl, when he thought he was handsome. And this one was handsome, with ink-dark curls falling over his forehead and golden skin, sun-warmed, his sleeves rolled up over muscular forearms. Instinctively, she glared back at him.

Unfazed by the glare, he slung the pack off his back and dug through it, extracting a pair of felt boots, which he held out to her. "Your foot is bleeding."

Sorel looked down and saw to her annoyance that it was true. He wasn't flirting; he was trying to sell her something.

She didn't want to acknowledge it, but on the other hand, she couldn't keep going barefoot. She slowed her pace to separate them from the old women and reluctantly took one of the hairpins from her pocket. "What will you give me for this? It's worth more than those cheap shoes."

The boy took the pin and inspected it closely, his eyebrows going up. He gave her a searching look, and Sorel clenched her fist, ready to grab it and run, but all he said was, "This is so expensive, you could have ten pairs of shoes."

"So?"

"So, anyone would think you'd stolen it."

Sorel snatched the pin back from him. "I didn't. It's my mother's."

The way he looked her over made her want to push him into the mud. "And what happened, God forbid, to your mother, that she can't send you out in the world with a good pair of boots?"

"None of your business," Sorel snapped.

The peddler spread his hands in a gesture of conciliation. "Listen, I'll take your trade, and I won't accuse you of stealing it—only, that's because I'm honest, and you're very young, and it's a mitzvah."

Sorel gave him the same once-over he'd given her, only putting as much hostility into the look as she could manage. "Not much younger than you."

He shrugged. "I'm Sam. Who are you?"

The name she'd pulled from nowhere for Old Rukhele came back easily. "Israel."

"Isserke. You haven't been on the road for long, have you? I'll give you the shoes for nothing and trade you advice for that pin instead. Snapping and biting only gets you so far— we Jews have to stick together."

Sorel wasn't convinced by the ahoves yisroel argument, but her feet hurt. She snatched the boots out of Sam's hand, and they stopped by the side of the road for her to put them on.

"Don't think I'm taking just advice for this," she told him when she offered him the hairpin again.

She expected more bargaining banter, but he just took a purse from his pocket and counted out a few coins. Sorel resented most of the education her father had insisted she have—what use was speaking German and playing the piano, in the real world—but in this moment she was grateful at least that she knew the value of material things.

Another little worry crept into the back of her mind: were there things she didn't know that would leave her vulnerable to being cheated?

You can always cheat people back, returned the part of her that had the confidence to run.

"Are you going to the wedding feast at the Great Synagogue?" Sam asked. "It's all anyone has been talking about on the road for days."

Sorel wished he wouldn't have taken their exchange as an invitation to a longer conversation. She shrugged, hunching her shoulders and turning away from him a little in hopes he'd give up and talk to someone else.

"The rebbe makes grand promises," said Sam, ignoring the signal. "I keep hearing that he's going to feed a thousand beggars. They say the bride's family is very wealthy. Everyone knows the name in these parts, but I've never stopped by them—Kalman the lumber merchant, isn't it? Do you know the family? I heard the daughter is very beautiful."

"They always say that about brides," Sorel scoffed. And what difference did it make? The rebbe's son wasn't marrying her because she was beautiful, which she wasn't. He was marrying her because her father was indeed wealthy, and she was marrying him because her wealthy father wanted to ensure the rebbe's blessings for himself forever. As far as she was concerned, it wasn't a marriage between a bride and groom at all: it was a marriage between two old widowers who spent their evenings together drinking brandy and deciding the fates of everyone around them with a sweep of their tipsy hands.

If the rebbe showed his face at the beggars' feast, she decided she would trip him into the mud.

"It's a simcha, anyway," said Sam, as if her resentment weren't clear in her voice. "And for me, a chance to rest. I've been on the road for weeks. It's been a long time since I visited Esrog, too—they say the city is full of troublemakers these days."

"Troublemakers?" Sorel had heard nothing of the sort, but then again, no one ever told her anything interesting. "What sort of troublemakers?"

"All the peasants in the villages insist the city is full of Jews who want to raise an army against the tsar."

"Don't be stupid. There's no such thing." Her father and the rebbe would never allow it—her father was always complaining about the minor rebellion of the Jewish smugglers who brought their goods up the river without the right stamps. Stamps he himself had paid good money for and kept paying good money to maintain. He certainly wouldn't have let anyone in his city entertain such a dangerous notion.

Sam laughed. "Well, I also heard that every Jew in Esrog sits on a throne of gold."

"That one's true," Sorel grumbled. "That's why all these bubbes are hobbling to a beggars' feast in their best rags."

Sam made a vague noise of agreement, and then to Sorel's relief, he let the conversation rest. They'd come to the river, and the bridge into the city was jammed with farmers' carts so they had to stop and wait. Sorel took the opportunity to sit down on a rock and let her feet rest, while Sam squatted nearby on the grass and watched each passerby with an alert expression. Looking for someone else to annoy, maybe. Sorel hoped he'd find them before it occurred to him to start asking questions about Isser's life.

The crowd waiting to cross the bridge was a mixture of peasants, poor Jews like the klogerin Rukhele who must be going to the wedding feast, and the more prosperous-looking young men in long coats whom Sorel suspected, with a twist of resentment, were the Hasidim of her arranged father-in-law. These students would be welcome at the feast, their dedication to learning making them effectively beggars even though they would have come from good families. She had eavesdropped on enough of her father's conversations with the rebbe to know that the Esroger Hasidim were selected from the respectable kind of Jews, the kind who could afford not to send their sons to mandatory state schools where young boys' heads were filled with peculiar notions and young girls' heads with rebellion.

Sorel had desperately wanted to go to a state school, but she was another variety of respectable Jew: the kind with a German governess, and no friends.

Now, she suppressed a flinch each time one of the boys in an Esroger hasid's coat glanced her way, but she refused to look away from them. None of them, not even those who'd dined as guests with her father, had ever looked at her face for more than the blink of an eye. She squashed her fear of being recognized with a ruthless determination to stare them all down. Isser, the wandering beggar boy, had no reason to avoid their gaze. Sorel decided that instead he ought to resent them. They had what he—she herself—did not, and they didn't even appreciate what they had.

Sam sprang to his feet as the knot at the end of the bridge cleared and traffic began to move again. Sorel followed him by instinct. At the gate were a pair of bored town guardsmen in garish uniforms, bright shades of blue and red clashing with each other. As Sam and Sorel passed, one grumbled to the other,

"Every time there's a problem it's these damn Jews coming in from the villages."

"How many festivals do they even have?" his companion agreed.

Sam grabbed Sorel's elbow and she jumped, realizing she'd fixed the guardsmen with a glare that could get her into trouble. She could feel Sam's eyes on the side of her face, but refused to acknowledge him, and kept walking. It wasn't like the guards had even noticed. They probably thought no one could understand them: they'd been speaking Russian. She shook Sam off as soon as they were past the gate.

"Your mother, may her memory be a blessing," Sam said, "Did she die recently?"

"What?"

"You said the hairpin was from your mother. You haven't been on the road long, and you have good jewelry, but no shoes. So you left home quickly, and recently. You didn't sell the pin to someone in your own village, so even though it was your mother's, they would think you were stealing—which means your father wouldn't have wanted you to sell it. Or else a stepfather? An older brother?"

"You're just guessing," said Sorel, bitter at how close he was to the truth. Still, he was wrong in ways that could help her. "My mother should have been granted a divorce and wasn't. Now she's dead and I've taken back her ketubah, that's all, not that it's your business. She wanted me to have a life, so I'm taking one for myself."

The last part was the truth, or Sorel hoped it was. She didn't remember enough of her mother to be certain.

"Since you've wrestled your life into your own hands, perhaps be more careful with it," said Sam. "Don't pick fights with men who carry sabres. For that advice, I owe you one kopek fewer for your hairpin."

"You owe me exactly what the pin was worth," Sorel told him. "And I'll fight you, since you've got no sabre."

Sam just laughed.

CHAPTER

2

THE GREAT SYNAGOGUE OF ESROG had once been a wooden building, painted in bright colors on the inside. In recent decades, it had been rebuilt in stone as a sort of symbol of the confidence and prosperity of the Esroger Jewish merchants, who got along well with the city authorities as long as the city authorities kept it clear in their heads that without the Jewish merchants there would be no city of Esrog.

Sorel had visited it once or twice on the High Holy Days, when her father wanted to make a grand appearance in the manner of a king, followed by his household. The women's gallery was upstairs, cramped and hidden behind carved wooden screens so that one could hardly see what was going on below, and in any case Sorel didn't even understand Hebrew. Her strongest memory from the synagogue was the slightly moldy scent that lived beneath the benches in the women's section, where she'd lain on her stomach and wished bitterly that any other little girl had bothered to come to services. If one had, she wasn't even sure she would have played nicely, but even a fight would have relieved the boredom.

While the rebbe was Hasidic, the Great Synagogue itself belonged to the maskilic city Jews, those like her father who spoke Russian, did business with gentiles, and studied modern sciences. Sorel's marriage to the rebbe's eldest son was intended to be a union between Hasidic and maskilic Jews to keep the city of Esrog from fracturing.

The courtyard in front of the modern stone edifice was crowded with tables today and loud as any village market. The assembled students and beggars could hardly keep themselves from reaching for the piles of loaves and roasted carp and chickens and potatoes: some were even sitting on their hands as they waited for the hamotzi to be said. Sorel passed through the crowd unremarked and unrecognized. She tried to squeeze herself between two old men, in a space too small for Sam to join her, but to her annoyance the elders moved over and Sam, somehow, wedged himself in at her elbow.

"What are we waiting for?" he asked.

"For a message from the rebbe, saying what is the luckiest time," replied one of the old men. "He is out in the woods, at Kalman's estate, and only he can speak to the angels to know the perfect hour for the union. He will send a runner."

Sam was looking at a plate of chicken with deep longing. "If only the angels understood how hungry one gets from walking."

Sorel couldn't help but agree. Her stomach, empty since yesterday, seemed ready to squirm up her throat and leap onto the table.

Just as it occurred to her that she didn't care what the rebbe thought and didn't care if she skipped a blessing either, there was a commotion in the street and a great cry of joy went up. She grabbed a piece of bread and stuffed it in her mouth while everyone was distracted, only then seeing that it was a Jew approaching on horseback, trotting between the crowds of revelers. He dismounted at the synagogue steps and went up to the elderly hasid who stood there, one of the rebbe's attendants whom she recognized from her father's house. The messenger's words were drowned out by cries of "Mazel tov!" and "May the rebbe live!" and so forth, but Sorel, who was watching carefully between bites of her blessingless bread, saw that the messenger and the rebbe's attendant both were frowning. They did not look as if they were discussing good mazel. They looked as if, perhaps, the messenger had come to explain that there was no wedding.

He finished speaking, and the elderly attendant stood for a moment with his hands folded, then unfolded them and stroked his beard. The cries of joy from the crowd were dying out as they grew impatient to eat again. Sam jostled Sorel's elbow and shook his head when she glanced at him, mouthing some sort of reproach at her for eating. Busybody!

At last, the rebbe's attendant lifted his hands for silence.

"The rebbe sends his blessing!" he cried. "Let us celebrate this feast for the long life and happiness of the bride and groom!"

Sorel stopped chewing. The messenger, still looking uncertain and anxious, handed the rebbe's attendant a loaf, and he called out the blessing to a raucous amen. The clatter of dishes and conversation rose again.

"What bride?" Sorel whispered, too low to be heard.

"You're lucky no one saw you eat without the blessing," said Sam, so close to her ear that she lifted her hand and swatted him. "You could have been trampled to death by pious alte-kackers."

"Shut up," she said, and elbowed him for good measure. "Stay out of my business."

How could there be a wedding without the bride? The rebbe's attendant must be covering for the awkwardness of the situation. Perhaps it was he who was afraid of being trampled. Sorel tried to keep eating as if nothing had happened, but the hunger had given way to gnawing, anxious curiosity. She had to know. But how could she ask?

The rebbe's attendant was whispering to the messenger again. Sorel got to her feet, her mind spinning out an excuse, a story—Mama, please forgive me for using you like this—but it was a good story, a good distraction, she thought. Only she wished her head was covered. Sam had a soft wool cap—she should have thought of it.

But it was too late, her feet were already carrying her to the synagogue steps, where the two men had been joined by a small group of others: a few of the rebbe's men, in dark coats, and a couple, incongruously, in the bright blue-and-red of the gentile guardsmen.

"A Jewish girl," the rebbe's attendant was saying as she came close, "tall, with red hair—not a beauty, but strong and healthy. What do you want?"

This was addressed to Sorel, a bit more harshly than she thought the old man intended. He softened his face as soon as he'd said it, folding his hands and smiling at her with the sweet detachment of an angel.

No one was giving her more than a disgusted sidelong glance, the distinct attitude of men who'd been interrupted and wanted to get back to business. Sorel, her heart leaping with an emotion she couldn't identify—was this terror or delight?—hung her head and wrung her hands.

"Reb Yid, you seem like a holy man—you must be one of the rebbe's tzadikim—I need to ask a favor, you see, my mother died, may she rest in peace; my mother died recently and I'm her kaddish, but I don't know the word—"

"Wait just one moment," said the rebbe's attendant. "Wait here."

He gave her a gesture like a man telling a dog to heel and turned back to the others. In Russian, he said, "We must find her before some misfortune falls on her. She is the rebbe's daughter-in-law. The wedding must take place. She can't have gotten far; she's only a girl, after all."

Sorel didn't wait to hear the rest. There had been no wedding, because indeed there was no bride. They only didn't want the embarrassment of the whole world knowing she'd escaped.

As she passed by the tables, she reached over the heads of the revelers to stuff her pockets with bread rolls and raisins and slipped out of the courtyard unnoticed. Her heart was singing now. The terror was gone, leaving the delight alone, as the men behind her broke ranks, going to search for a tall Jewish girl with red hair—whose face they'd just looked at, and not seen.

Sorel Kalmans did not exist.

SHE NEEDED TO SELL the hairpins. Those, aside from her face, were the most unique thing she had. She hated to part with them, but then, they were expensive. She could live on them for awhile. She'd need to cover her hair—boys covered their heads anyway—and someone who bothered to really look

THE FORBIDDEN BOOK

would see how badly she'd shorn it in the darkness, with a knife and the dedication of panic. And then? Anything. Anything! Isser Jacobs could go where he wanted, could do anything.

Isser walked with the confidence of one who knew the streets of Esrog well. Sorel had not walked these streets: when her father brought her to the festivals, she had ridden in a carriage. But now she walked with long strides, her hands in her pockets, and whistled a little song as she watched for the sign of a pawn shop or jeweler. The fox who had sprung the trap last night now found itself outside the farmer's walls, savoring the wide-open world.

A few twists and turns brought her to a street in the Jewish district whose shops advertised used clothing and furniture. The first shop Sorel looked into had a woman behind the counter, mending a seam on a pair of trousers. Sorel felt somehow that a woman might see through her more easily than a man, so she continued on to the next, which was selling a jumble of clothing out of stacks of orange crates. The shopkeeper here was an old man in spectacles who gave her the same assessing look as Sam when she offered her hairpins, but he didn't ask aloud if she'd stolen them. Sorel bargained for a hat, new thicker socks, a satchel to carry things in, and tied up the rest of her money in her stocking. At the last moment, she thought to purchase a tallit katan, so that the tzitzis at her hips could help her disguise as a boy.

Trying out a new story, she told the old man that she was an orphan, and she was going to Odessa to find some distant relatives of her mother's. He either believed her or couldn't be bothered to care, merely grumbled half-hearted responses; she left him polishing her hairpins with a silk handkerchief.

She hid in an alleyway to wriggle into the undershirt without taking off her shirt, tucked the loose strands of her hair into the cap, and started walking again with a spring in her step. The morning fog had burned off, and the blue sky reflected her mood. She felt she could do anything, go anywhere. Why not go to Odessa? She could lose herself entirely there. She'd take a coach to the railroad, and then a train—she had seen a train, once, her father had taken her to watch it hurtle by on a newly opened stretch of track. She remembered the rush of it and remembered also that her father had been displeased by it. That night he had one of his long discussions with the rebbe, sequestered in his study with endless glasses of brandy. Sorel had not understood then, and did not understand now, what had upset the old men so much, but she liked the idea of taking the train away from her father and her wedding. It would be another jab at her father.

She was taking turns randomly, not entirely sure of the direction to the coaching inns on the main road out of the city, and did not notice at first when someone cut across her path. She moved to the side automatically, assuming he meant to pass her by, but he sidestepped to block her way out of the narrow, cobblestone back alley. It was a young man, a gentile close to her own age and dressed in the uniform of a guard but without the garish coat.

Sorel stopped and glared at him. "What do you want?"

"How did you come back here?" He'd planted his feet in a stance that said she'd have to fight him to get past.

"I walked," she said. She didn't necessarily want to pick a fight with a guard—that is, the part of her that was sensible didn't—but if he'd recognized her, she wouldn't be reluctant to punch him in the face. "Listen, I'm leaving the city, so whatever your problem is, find someone else to take it out on."

The young man made a grab for her, and she skipped backward, her hand curling around the handle of her knife.

"You're supposed to be dead," he said.

Sorel stopped. "What?"

"God damn Borysko," said the guard. "He said he'd killed you. Where is it? Do you still have it?"

Some instinct made Sorel look over her shoulder, and a chill went through her as she saw that while they'd been talking, two more men had come up the alley behind her. They were also gentiles without jackets and with sleeves rolled up as if they already had the intention to fight.

She decided in that moment that she didn't care what the man was talking about, or who he'd mistaken her for. There was no point in waiting to find out.

"Stop him!" the guard shouted as she leapt for the gap between the two newcomers—they'd been expecting her to run for the easier escape. She almost made it past them, but one grabbed the tail of her long coat and yanked her back. She struck out blindly with the knife and heard a gratifying howl of pain. All three men were yelling now, cursing her and each other. Someone caught her arm and threw her to the ground. She shielded her face with her arms and rolled, struck out the knife again, and felt it sink into something solid, flesh or leather. The guard kicked back at her, and the knife flew from her hand, clattering onto the cobbles out of reach. She thought for a moment that he meant to stomp on her face, but instead one of the other two grabbed her by the back of her collar and hauled her to her feet, pinning her arm as she tried to jab him with her elbow. The largest of the three, fair-haired and blocky with the muscles of someone who did manual labor, was glaring and nursing a cut that ran down his arm from elbow to wrist. She felt some grim satisfaction that she'd at least made him bleed. The guardsman, clearly the ringleader, stared her down as she struggled in the third man's grip.

"Where is it?" he repeated his nonsensical question from before.

"I don't know what you're talking about," Sorel said.

"Of course you don't, you damned snake," said the guard. He shifted his stance, uncomfortable, and Sorel saw that he too was bleeding, a dark stain spreading on the calf of his trousers. If she could only get free to run, she thought, she could run faster.

The man was still talking. "You're a fine liar, Isser, and you've led us on a fine goose hunt, but I'm tired of chasing you. You can tell us now, or we can ask your little Jewess— what's her name? Adela Pinsker? I know where she lives, Isser. I found her letters in your room. So sweet! A girl with real thoughts in her head. Wouldn't you be sorry if I had to talk to Adela? Wouldn't you rather we finish it here, now?"

Sorel blinked at him. Isser, that was her name, the name she'd given—had he overheard her talking to Rukhele, or to Sam? He must have heard her give the name and mistaken her for another Isser. Maybe all Jews looked the same to him.

She opened her mouth to tell him she didn't know anyone called Adela, but the words died on her tongue at the sound of a deep, rumbling growl—a growl that raised all the hairs on the back of her neck. She saw the same fear reflected in the men's eyes as they turned, looking for the source of the sound.

A great black dog crouched in the mouth of the alley, shoulders low to the ground, teeth bared. Its eyes were light, almost wolf-gold. It could have been mistaken for a wolf, if not for its dropped ears.

"What the hell—" the guardsman began to say, but the words were lost in a shout of alarm as the dog sprang from its position and hit him with the full force of its leap, knocking him over. The man holding Sorel staggered back. His grip loosened, and she tore out of his grasp and threw herself down the alley, looking for the knife. Instinct told her she shouldn't turn her back on the dog, but she couldn't make herself look. The guardsman was screaming. The third man, the fair-haired one, ran past Sorel as she picked up the knife. His eyes were wide with panic. Sorel glanced back and saw the dog with its jaws around the ankle of the man who'd been holding her, knocking him off his feet and dragging him. The guards-man lay on his back, staring with wide, blank eyes at the sky, blood pooling around his head.

She moved backward, step by step, the knife clutched tightly in front of her chest. She did not think she could outrun the dog. She watched it plant a great, heavy paw on the back of the second man and shut her eyes as its jaws closed on the back of his neck. The cobbles were uneven under her feet as she took another step backward, then another, eyes shut, the sound of her own breath loud in her ears.

There was no thud of paws chasing after her. She did not feel the hot breath of the wolf on her face. The growling had ceased.

She stumbled backward out of the alley into the startling heat of the sunlight. She felt as if she had just stepped out from underwater—suddenly, human voices were loud around her, people going about their ordinary business.

When she opened her eyes, she saw no dog in the alley. There were two men lying still on the stones, and there was Sorel, with the knife in her hand.

A woman passing by with a basket of leeks gave her an odd look and Sorel fumbled the knife back into its sheath and wiped her hands on her coat, though she saw no trace of blood on them, only dirt and sweat. What had she just seen? What had she just done?

"Isserke!" a voice called a cheerful greeting. "I was wondering where you'd disappeared to."

It was Sam, grinning, his peddler's pack slung casually over one shoulder. Despite herself, Sorel was glad to see him. He seemed solid and real, his warm golden skin belonging firmly to the world of sun and human voices.

"I was looking for a coach," she said, her voice hoarse. She moved toward him, forcing herself not to look back into the alleyway. "I got turned around."

ISSER JACOBS came home to his room from the print shop one day in the spring to find Kalman Senderovich's gentile stableboy, Ostap, waiting for him with a message.

"He wants to talk to you. He's at the Great Synagogue."

The boy was Isser's own age, illiterate, and incurious, but all his own shortcomings only made him happier when he got to order Isser around, wielding the authority of Kalman Senderovich like the tsar's scepter.

"Talk to me about what?" said Isser. Kalman did not usually bother meeting with him. It was beneath the dignity of Esrog's single most important Jew to speak face-to-face with a poor orphan and—let it not be spoken aloud—a criminal. Usually, the gentile boy just brought him messages written in stiff Yiddish and stood around looking impatient while Isser read them.

"You think he tells me about what? Just hurry up. I've been waiting for ages."

Isser hadn't eaten, and he didn't much relish the walk all the way across the Jewish Quarter to the Great Synagogue, but he wasn't going to complain to Ostap. The boy seemed to think Isser was his competition somehow, and though Isser always told himself he wouldn't rise to the aggravation, he still didn't like to give Ostap the upper hand. So he turned on his heel and walked right back into the stable-yard, on his tired feet, so that Ostap had to jog after him.

Kalman Senderovich, of course, wasn't simply waiting in idleness for someone as insignificant as Isser. Let there be no respect for the fact that Isser never told him no: Kalman the lumber merchant would never have considered it possible that someone should refuse him.

He was conducting business, not in the synagogue itself, God forbid, but in the inn next door at the great room in the back with the other members of Esrog's Jewish governing council, the kahal. Isser was left to sit in the hall, waiting, while Ostap irritatingly refused to go back out to the stables. Instead he joined Isser on the bench and downed glass after glass of hot cider, as if he never had a chance to get drunk on Kalman's estate and as if he didn't have the horses to look after or even a carriage to drive. Isser couldn't be bothered to keep track of which petty responsibilities fell to Ostap on what occasions, but he remembered at least once the other boy had tried to impress him by mentioning that Kalman had him drive.

"You heard his girl's getting married?" Ostap asked, after they'd been sitting awhile and Isser had steadfastly refused to speak to him. "That's real news, that is. No one in the city will know that yet."

Isser had seen Kalman's daughter once or twice. A tall girl, bony. He remembered thick eyebrows. Once, he'd been leaving Kalman's study—on a rare occasion when he had actually been on the estate—and they'd passed each other in the hall and she'd twitched her skirt away from him as if she expected him to soil it. Another time, he'd sold her a chapter of a novel for a markup she didn't notice.

He did not much care if Kalman's daughter got married.

Ostap the stable-boy didn't care if Isser was interested or not. The important thing was that spreading fresh gossip gave one power. He went on, "You'll never believe who she's marrying, either. The rebbe's son."

Isser turned his head and mentally kicked himself for showing a reaction. Ostap was smirking at him. But he had to know.

"Not Shulem-Yontif?"

"God knows," said Ostap. "How many sons has he got?"

"Only one old enough to marry," Isser conceded, though truth be told even Shulem-Yontif was a bit young—he was fifteen, the girl was seventeen or eighteen. Not the youngest anyone ever got engaged. But these were modern times, and Kalman was a modern Jew. Isser would have thought he'd marry the girl to some maskil or a rich merchant from Odessa. What did he want with a hasid for a son-in-law? "What kind of marriage is that?"

Ostap laughed. "What? Were you hoping he'd make you his son-in-law? You're less than dirt to him."

"It doesn't seem the kind of match he would have made, that's all," said Isser.

The stable-boy let him sit for a minute wondering about it, just to flex his own superior knowledge. Isser swallowed his pride and prompted, "You're such a trusted servant. I just thought he would have told you why."

"Maybe," said Ostap, glowing. "Maybe not. If he did, I wouldn't be telling the world about it. That's Reb Kalman's own business, isn't it."

And Shulem-Yontif's business, and the girl's, Isser thought. What was her name? Soreh. The princess. God, she'd eat Shuli alive. "You can borrow my knife, if you like."

The knife had been a source of contention between Isser and Ostap for nearly a year now, since Kalman Senderovich gave it to Isser with the warning to watch his back about the city and the order to never breathe a word to anyone about the lumber merchant's business. Isser had taken this as a sort of threat, a tacit suggestion that he should cut his own throat before betraying Kalman's confidence. Every time he touched the decorated leather sheath, it gave him a chill. But the print shop had been raided twice this year, and sometimes he had a sense of being followed as he walked through the city. And so, he kept it with him.

Ostap saw it as a sign of unearned favor. To him, it was something beautiful that Isser did not appreciate. His eyes shined as Isser handed it to him, hilt first, and he slid it from its case to admire the glow of the lamplight on the blade.

"You don't take care of her," he said. "Look, the leather will crack if you don't season it."

"To hell with the leather," said Isser. "Why's Kalman's daughter marrying the rebbe's son?"

"Twisted his arm, didn't they," said Ostap. He picked a loose thread out of his trousers and tested the edge of the knife, looking pleased with the result. "The kahal's about to mutiny. No one listens to Kalman anymore. All your lazy Jews here in the city with no jobs, looking for handouts. Well who gives them the handouts? Their rebbe, that's who. Handouts, and promises that they can bring your Messiah."

"What Messiah wants to visit Esrog?" Isser grumbled.

"Anyway, Reb Kalman knows what's good for the city, but he can't get any of those superstitious fools to listen. So what does he do? He says to the rebbe, here, you can have your miracles, feed your cripples, and whatever else you want. But you'll do it as my daughter's father-in-law, and it's my name people will be repeating when they talk about how the wedding saved Esrog from ruin. Clever, isn't he? Clever son of a bitch."

Isser propped his chin in his hands, frowning at the opposite wall. He had a sinking feeling that Kalman's business with him today had something to do with the wedding. It wouldn't be *get me a copy of this book, with a fake censor's stamp on it so it looks legal*. It would be something complicated and strange.

Before he could come up with a guess, the door of the back room opened and the men of the kahal filed out, sharing their own gossip as they went and paying the boys no heed. Ostap slid Isser's knife into his pocket, put down his empty glass, and slunk after them, getting himself out of the way in case Kalman caught him idling.

Isser waited until the last of the elders was gone and went in to Kalman Senderovich. The lumber merchant was sitting alone at the table, making a note in his community ledger.

There was a decimated platter of rugelach in front of him, so Isser took one without asking and sat down without being asked.

"Ah, Israel," said Kalman, barely glancing up and entirely ignoring the rudeness. "Good. I need you to steal something."

CHAPTER

3

SAM CHEERFULLY took on the task of guiding Sorel to a coaching inn. She followed him without really listening as he chattered about the wedding feast, the rebbe's blessings, and the tzedakah that had been handed out. Her hands were cold as ice, and she found herself shaking. When she closed her eyes, she saw the blank gaze of the guardsman with his throat torn out. Where had the dog gone? How could she have imagined such a thing? But how could it have been real?

She stumbled, and Sam caught her by the elbow.

"You're exhausted," he said, steering her to the side of the street. "You left the feast in a hurry, didn't you? You need to eat."

Sorel, trembling, could say nothing. She felt she might pass out.

Sam guided her inside a coffeehouse with a card in the window that declared it to be kosher. There he sat her down in a corner and brought her a mug of a strong, bitter drink with a plate of kugel. She drank the coffee, wrapping her hands around it and trying to stop the tremors. The kugel she didn't touch. Sam sat watching her, his gaze steady, quiet for once, until she'd drained the cup.

"I know who you are," he said at last.

Sorel had been staring at the table, her eyes unfocused. Her gaze snapped now to Sam's. She didn't think she could run again. He was between her and the door in any case—it hadn't occurred to her that she was trapped.

"You don't," she whispered, too tired to put much fight into it.

"I do." He bent down and opened the peddler's pack that lay by his feet. After a moment of searching he extracted a cheaply printed pamphlet with Hebrew letters and a woodblock illustration on the cover. Sam flipped it over and slid it across the table to her, tapping with one finger on a handwritten note on the blank back page. "You're Isser the printer's apprentice, aren't you? I've been looking for you."

Sorel's head spun. The note was an address, here in Esrog—for Isser Jacobs.

Sam leaned forward and lowered his voice. "Those men who were following you, they wanted something from you? Do they know you've been printing these in secret?"

Sorel picked up the pamphlet, reading the note again. She felt dizzy, the letters swimming in front of her eyes.

"What men?" Her voice was barely a croak.

"Three men followed you when you left the feast," said Sam. "Goyim."

"I don't know what they wanted," she said. "They were looking for someone else. I didn't know them."

"But you are Isser Jacobs?"

"Not this Isser Jacobs!" She shoved the pamphlet back across the table to him. "It's just a name! There can be more than one!"

Sam frowned and checked the note a second time, as if he expected it to clarify the situation.

Sorel, suddenly starving, grabbed the plate of kugel and shoved a bite in her mouth, chewing desperately. "I am not a printer's apprentice, and whichever Isser printed that, he needs to take care of his own business, because I'm already tired of his people. I'm leaving Esrog, I'm going to Odessa, and I'm never coming back—I'll go to France if I have to! I hate this place."

"Lower your voice, please," said Sam. "And don't talk with your mouth full. I was supposed to meet Isser here, in the city. You don't have to pretend with me. Just having the pamphlets is enough of a crime, but it would be easy enough to prove that I've been selling them, too. Any court would simply assume that I have! So you have nothing to hide from me."

"I am not the person you're looking for," said Sorel. She swallowed the last of the kugel and picked up the pamphlet. She didn't recognize the address, but she knew approximately where it ought to be in relation to the Great Synagogue. The look of the pamphlet jogged her memory—a boy who came to the estate sometimes. He'd been soaking wet from the rain when she ran into him in the kitchen, gossiping with the cooks. He'd sold her an installment of a Russian novel on the same paper, and at the time, she hadn't bothered to remember him. Was *that* why the name "Israel Jacobs" had come to her? "Why don't we go to his home and prove it? I want a word with him anyway. He owes me—he owes me."

She didn't know what Isser owed her. Perhaps she would just give him a slap in the face and curse his ancestors for naming him something so simple, so uncreative that she could mistake it for a name she hadn't heard. She had no one else to direct her feelings toward, so he'd have to do. Sam left a few coins on the table and followed her out of the coffeehouse, uncomplaining, an infuriating tilt of amusement to his mouth as if he thought she was putting on a performance.

The Isser from the pamphlet lived in an alley off the Street of Bookmakers in the Jewish district, a neighborhood of crooked medieval streets behind the Great Synagogue. It was a building with a courtyard, the sort of place where each room was rented out to a family and every window hung with drying laundry. There was a print shop on the first floor in the front selling women's prayer books. Isser Jacobs lived over the stables in the back, a room up a narrow exterior staircase to what had once been a hayloft. The stables themselves must now house the presses. The thumping of equipment shook the building with each step as Sam and Sorel climbed the stairs.

It was immediately clear that all was not well in Israel Jacobs's rooms. At the top of the staircase, Sorel's foot collided with something that clattered on the floor, and when Sam picked it up, cradling it in his hand like a small fragile animal, she saw that it was a cheap brass mezuzah case, twisted from being torn from the wall. The door was ajar, the lock broken and hanging loosely.

Sorel drew her knife and carefully pushed the door open. Sam was searching the floor for the mezuzah scroll and didn't stop her. Inside, the room had been ransacked. It was a chaos of broken furniture covered in stove ash and loose feathers from the disemboweled bed. No one was there now, and she thought no one had been there for a while. The heavy air suggested that no one had moved through the space in some time.

Sam followed her inside, tucking the rescued scroll and its case into his vest pocket. "I wasn't the only one looking for you, no?"

"Not for me." Sorel nudged a pile of clothing with her foot and found a broken plate and a book in German, facedown. Reading German was impressive for a printer's apprentice. Most boys she knew read only in Hebrew, and even then, not well. Surely he hadn't been printing in German? As far as she knew, it was only legal to print religion. "For the real Isser."

"Lucky you weren't here," said Sam, reaching past her to pick the book up. He gave it a gentle shake to dislodge the dirt and closed it with care, though it wasn't a prayer book. It looked to Sorel like a novel. "Whoever it was, I don't think they found what they wanted, but they could have just left things alone. Instead of breaking everything."

He kept picking things up, folding the clothes, and setting a few more books on the table. Sorel stood where she was, feeling useless and uneasy. It wasn't like she had to keep the name she'd stumbled on by accident. She could just change it, nothing was stopping her. She could walk away from whatever was going on here and go back to planning her new life far away.

But already two people had mistaken her for him. And someone wanted to hurt him. And Sorel knew how it felt to be on the run.

"What was it you wanted him for?" she asked, her voice faraway in her own ears.

"He's been selling me those pamphlets," said Sam. "Or anyway, the person who sold them to me said Isser Jacobs was the source."

Sorel hadn't bothered to actually read the pamphlet. Sam seemed to realize this, because when she didn't respond, he continued, "They're politics, translated into Yiddish. Stories about Jewish Emancipation in Europe. Things like that, that the censors wouldn't allow. Someone must have found out about it."

"Then those men who were following me," said Sorel. "One of them was a city guard."

"If they haven't found the other Isser, he'll be in trouble when they do," said Sam. He gave her a look as if he expected something from her in response. She wondered if he still thought she was putting on an act.

Then she remembered something else. "The ones who found me—one of them said something about a girl. A Jewish girl, what was the name?"

One of the men had run off, she stopped herself from saying. She didn't want Sam to ask what happened to the other two. She preferred not to think about it herself; every time she did, she felt a wave of nausea.

She couldn't remember the girl's name.

"Look for something that points to her," Sam suggested. "We can find her first and warn her."

It was enough to shake her out of her stupor. Better to be doing something, at least, while she tried to shake the memory loose. Together they brushed dust and ashes off of books and broken plates, an ink pot, a milk jug. Sam found a siddur and stopped for a minute to clean it more carefully, whispering too low for Sorel to hear. She felt the creeping sensation that she was tracing the steps of the ones who'd broken into

Isser's room in the first place, trying to turn back time. When she checked inside the stove, just to be thorough, she found a bundle of letters that were crumpled and torn but hadn't managed to burn. Someone had tossed them on top of the coals, and they'd smothered the flame instead of catching.

"Adela Pinsker," she said, skimming over them. They seemed innocent, mostly short notes about the weather and the health of family members, but at least she recognized the name. "It says she lives in Kuritsev."

Kuritsev was another village on the outskirts of Esrog, if she remembered right. In the opposite direction from home, which would be a relief.

"Then we'll go to Kuritsev," said Sam.

Sorel didn't argue. She had forgotten that she wanted to be rid of him.

As URGENT AS IT FELT to warn Adela Pinsker that she was in trouble, Sorel's feet were paining her terribly, and Sam noticed the limp. He suggested that they rest for the night and set off in the morning. Sorel expected that they would have to find rooms, to sleep like real people, but Sam brought her back across the river to the cemetery where she'd run into Old Rukhele. Apparently, this was how a peddler slept: wrapped up in his coat, in the grass, after a meal of cold kugel that he'd kept wrapped up in a handkerchief in his pocket. Sorel shared the buns that she'd stolen from the wedding feast, and

Sam picked the raisins out and threw them to the crows, who hopped circles around the two of them croaking "Rekh! Rekh!" while they ate.

"Aren't you afraid that a ghost will find you, sleeping in places like this?" Sorel asked, the foolish question taking her mind off Isser, and Adela, and the rebbe's men looking for her.

"Not really," said Sam. Then, not reassuringly, "In any case, there are corpses enough outside of cemeteries. You never know where death will find you. Why not go where you expect it?"

Sorel made a face. She could not say that she had ever found death where she expected it. On the other hand, he had a point—the cemetery was peaceful and smelled of moss and flowering trees, and the grass was warm this late in the day, holding onto some afternoon heat.

"My father is a kohen," she said. "He wouldn't be pleased with me for sitting here."

"And for running away from home he'd be pleased?" said Sam. "Forget what your father likes, that's my advice. And if you're worried about the ghosts, here—this will protect you."

He dug around in his pack and found a little silk pouch embroidered with letters that she thought might be a holy name. Into this, he placed the mezuzah scroll from Isser's apartment and held it out to her.

"I sell a lot of amulets," he explained, at the look she was giving his pack. "And the scroll must have been lonely, lying there abandoned, don't you think?"

Sorel didn't think the poor lonely scroll had done much for Isser Jacobs. She was now remembering that the men who'd come after her had said he should be dead—maybe there was no real Isser anymore. But she said none of this to Sam, who was watching her expectantly.

Instead, she took the pouch with the mezuzah and tucked it into the pocket of her coat, where she felt its weight on her hip as she curled up to sleep.

CHAPTER

SOREL RAN ON FOUR PAWS, slipping between tree roots and under brambles. In the dream she was certain something chased her, but she didn't know what it was. She knew only the scent of damp loam, the clicks and squeaks of little animals warning each other of a predator as she passed by, and the satisfaction of her own clever agility, the way she landed sure-footed after every leap. This forest was old, getting older the farther she ran, the trees looming high above her, the moon swimming in a misty sky. She landed on a mossy boulder and stopped for a moment, sniffing the air. She was looking for something, she remembered. Not the things that squeaked and scuttled in the underbrush. Something distant, something complicated.

A dog barked in the distance, and she pressed herself to the surface of the stone, panting. She could not be seen. She could not be heard. He could not smell her fear.

She crept from the height and searched the roots of the tree, looking for a crevice to tuck herself into when she could not keep running. The rich scent of the earth would disguise her. Here, this place smelled inviting, rich, alive. A scent that would fool the dog's nose and keep her safe.

The fox tucked her tail and crept into a space beneath an ancient beech. The baying of the dog came closer and closer, until she heard his heavy paws in the mast on the forest floor, circling. She heard the huffing of his breath, closer and closer.

But he did not smell her. He passed by, a looming shadow between her and the starlight, and the sound of his paws grew faint and fainter, until his voice sounded again as a distant howl.

She crept from her hiding place, lifting her paws with care, taking sips of the night breeze to clear the heady scent of underground from her nose.

"Sorel," said a voice she was sure she knew from somewhere. "Is that you?"

Sorel, the fox, cowered back toward the hole in the ground, but the scent of the newcomer was reassuring, familiar as the voice. He was a pale smudge in her vision at first, and then he knelt in the leaves and reached out a hand for her. Creeping forward, she recognized him immediately.

It was her own face. The face of Sorel Kalmans. The voice was hers, too. Yet, with the logic of dreams, she was certain it was a boy, borrowing the face and the voice while Sorel herself looked back at him with the fox's eyes.

"It is you, isn't it?" the boy whispered, uncertain, hopeful. "Please, you have to find me."

The dog barked, suddenly close, and Sorel's eyes snapped open.

SAM WAS AWAKE and watching her. The cemetery was full of morning fog, the sky just starting to turn light. Sorel didn't ask if the bad dream had been obvious—she didn't want to hear the answer.

She got up without speaking and wrapped her coat more tightly, staggering into the woods for a moment alone. She couldn't shake the feeling of being followed. Every little sound of the woods was magnified by the foggy morning, as if she still had the fox's hearing. She couldn't shake the image of the boy with her own face, and the cold dread at the thought of him reaching out to touch her, as if some instinct told her the touch would be poison.

She thought the boy had been Isser. The real Isser. She knew it the same way she'd known he was a boy even though he looked like her, the same way it had felt natural to run on a fox's four paws.

She was glad the dog had woken her. The thought of what message Isser might have for her hollowed out a pit in her stomach and made her shudder with more than cold.

She went to the river and washed the cold sweat from her face. When she came back, Sam had wrapped tfillin and was swaying silently in the middle of a circle of perplexed and sleepy crows. Sorel tugged uncomfortably at the tzitzis on her own hips and wondered if he'd notice if she didn't pray like a man. Surely some beggars just didn't have the will for it. She decided that Isser Jacobs was not pious. He had a grievance against his father in the story she'd given Sam. Maybe the grievance extended to God as well.

Sam finished davening and tucked the tfillin away in a pocket of his peddler's bag. "Kuritsev is east along the main road. You'll warm up quicker if we start walking at once."

Sorel tried to shrug away her shivers, irritated that they'd been so obvious. Her stomach was griping at her for break-fast, but she'd eaten everything she stole from the wedding feast the day before and didn't want to ask if Sam had any-thing. She was a little reluctant to take the main road, expos-ing herself to whatever searchers were after her from her father and the rebbe, but that too, she couldn't say.

Instead, she kept her head down and followed Sam, who walked not quickly but at a steady, determined pace, as if nothing could stop or slow him. Sorel's feet hurt and her back hurt and she felt bruised all over. She found herself dozing on her feet and dreaming of a hot bath, but whenever she closed her eyes, she saw Isser looking at her with her own wide eyes.

He'll be in Kuritsev, she told herself. He must have run from Esrog to warn Adela of trouble, and we'll find them both there. We'll get there ahead of whoever's looking, and everything will be fine.

The pounding hooves of a troop of horses woke her from her haze. Sam was tugging at her elbow to get her off the side of the road, standing knee-deep in nettles. The group were uniformed soldiers, men from the city garrison most likely, but coming from the direction of Sorel's home. They cantered past and then slowed upon seeing Sam and Sorel. For a moment there was a fierce, angry look on Sam's face, his lip curled in hatred, but he smoothed it into his customary easy grin as the leader of the group approached them.

"You there!" Sorel recognized this man, or at least recognized his well-groomed mustache. She'd seen him at her father's dinners, one of the many men she was supposed to politely converse with while making no real connection—never to a gentile. It was very European, very sophisticated, for a girl to speak to officers, and her father encouraged the sophistication but wouldn't dream of anything more.

She kept her head down, standing behind Sam's shoulder and imitating the sullen, nervous posture she'd seen the rebbe's son, her fiancé, adopt whenever he and she had been in the same room. Every inch of the posture said she had nothing interesting to say.

"Good morning," said Sam, in passable Russian. Sorel heard the Yiddish accent in it and was a little surprised that he didn't speak better. "Can I help you?"

"Have you seen a Jewish girl on the road?" said the officer.

Sorel shifted her feet, then stopped herself. She could not make it obvious that she was preparing to run. Sam would notice—he had let go of her elbow, but he was standing very close to her.

"A Jewish girl?" said Sam. "I haven't seen any girls this morning, more's the pity."

"You, boy," said the officer, and repeated himself when Sorel didn't respond. "You, have you seen anything?"

"He's been with me," said Sam. "And his Russian is bad."

Lying, and Sorel thought he knew he was lying. Jews sticking together, or whatever he'd said yesterday. She'd have to tell him she didn't need to be protected—but later, when it felt more true.

"Well, if you see or hear of a girl on her own, there's a reward in it," said the officer. "A Jewish girl, eighteen years old, tall. She's gone missing, and her father, Kalman the lumber merchant, is searching for her."

"How terrible," said Sam. "But I'm sorry, I've heard of nothing."

The officer huffed out a breath of annoyance, as if Sam's ignorance were a deliberate slight, and tapped his heels to his horse's sides. The animal leapt forward, and a moment later, the men were gone.

"Kalman the lumber merchant's daughter," said Sam. "How can she be missing? We were just at her wedding feast."

"Maybe a dybbuk took her," croaked Sorel, nervously.

"True, it happens to brides sometimes, God forbid," said Sam. "I was afraid they were looking for Adela Pinsker."

"Right." Sorel picked a thorn out of her trouser leg, avoiding eye contact. "We should hurry."

KURITSEV WAS on the other side of a small range of hills, a prosperous shtetl scarcely five miles from the railroad, as Sam explained to Sorel while they walked. He seemed fascinated by the railroad and gave her a lot of details about its construction, most of which she didn't bother to listen to. Apparently, it was the fault of the hills that the railroad hadn't come to Esrog. As far as Sorel was concerned, it was the fault of the hills that she was hot and hungry and tired before the sun had even hit its zenith.

The town itself was well-kept, with neat fences along the square and flowers growing by the gutters rather than the sucking mud that plagued Sorel's hometown. It must have been home to a mix of Jews and gentiles, because a little church with a spire faced the synagogue across the square. A small group of old men sat on stools outside the synagogue, smoking pipes and conversing, even a Christian among them holding his own. The conversation was about cattle. Sam interrupted them to ask after the Pinsker family while Sorel kicked at rocks and tried to shake the sense that the cheerful little town was hiding something from her.

"Pinsker's the dairyman," said one of the elders, pointing with his pipe. "A hundred daughters, he has—God forbid."

"A hundred?" said Sam, mildly startled.

"Well, five or six," said the old man. "Now, did you come from Esrog way? What's this about the lumber merchant's daughter? The rebbe's daughter-in-law-to-be? She's missing, is it?"

The old men, even the Christian, seemed very eager to get all of the details, leaping almost at once to the catastrophic implications of breaking the wedding.

"If demons got to the rebbe's daughter-in-law, God forbid, they could get to any of us."

"How can a girl just disappear?"

"Did you hear anything of it?"

Sorel didn't stay to listen to whatever gossip Sam might have to share. She knew exactly how a girl could disappear, and she didn't mind if it brought misfortune, God forbid, on the heads of all Israel, as long as she wasn't there to partake in it. What mattered to her was finding Adela Pinsker before anyone else did.

It was easy enough to find the dairyman's cottage, following the vague direction of the pipe. It was a pretty, two-story building with cheerful floral window boxes and a sign carved into a whimsical caricature of some sort of dairy animal she couldn't identify with certainty. Sorel hesitated at the door, finding it difficult to connect this lovely place with the alleyway back in Esrog and the tearing of the black dog's jaws.

Before she could bring herself to knock, the door opened sharply, revealing a pair of eyes glaring at her from inside. She took a step backward under the force of the look.

"What are you doing here?" said the girl in the doorway. She was shorter than Sorel—most girls were—and round in places where Sorel was angular, with a sweet, heart-shaped face. Yet there was a core of steel in her posture. She was holding a cheese knife just behind the fold of her skirts, where only a glint of sun off the blade alerted Sorel to its presence. "What do you want?"

"I'm looking for—" Sorel started to say, stammering, but the girl interrupted her.

"Where have you been, Isser?"

Sorel bit her tongue. What was everyone seeing when they were looking at her? She wished suddenly that she had a mirror. Had Isser stolen her face in the waking world, just like in her dreams? But she still had breasts. She could feel them, a constant, bothersome feeling at the back of her mind.

"I'm not Isser," she whispered at last. She couldn't make herself lie to this girl.

"Excuse me?"

"You're Adela, aren't you? Can I come in? It's a very strange story."

Adela gave her a long, hard look. "I don't know why I thought it was him. Trick of the light. Who are you, then?"

"I came for Isser," said Sorel. "To warn you—only I don't know exactly what I'm warning you about, and I hoped I'd find him here already. I'm, my name is—" She cast about for a suitable name, struggled for long enough that Adela's eyebrows went up. "Alter." Then she remembered Sam, and that she'd have to explain the change in names if he called her by the one he knew. "Israel Alter, I'm a friend. Or anyway, Isser's enemies tried to kill me yesterday, so I'd like to be your friend."

Adela looked skeptical still, but her posture relaxed a little, and she took half a step back. Sorel's knees went shaky with relief.

"I have another friend with me," she added, "Sam. He's been buying pamphlets."

As if the name summoned him, he appeared from out of the corner so she was able to point him out. Adela inspected him, leaning out the door, but seemed to find nothing strange about him. Sorel felt an odd spike of jealousy. Did his handsome face excuse his lack of invitation?

Adela let them both in, and even put down the knife she'd been holding the whole time. The house was just as cheerful and clean inside as it was outside, with a polished wooden floor in the front and tile in the kitchen in back.

"Everyone else went to the cattle market," Adela said. "It's the only time I'm alone in the house."

"Is that why you were so cautious?" Sorel asked.

"I was cautious because I thought I'd seen a ghost!" said Adela. She seemed to have shaken whatever fear that caused, however, because she turned her back on them now and took bread and cheese from a cupboard and started setting the table as if by habit. "And because I had some men come by looking for Isser before. Last month. I've been waiting for them to come by again—or for him."

"So you haven't seen him?" said Sam. "I hoped I could find him. I have good customers for him."

Adela shook her head. She set a teapot and cups on the table and sat down. Her shoulders tensed. "It's been weeks."

"Do you know what he did?" Sorel asked. "I mean, why they're looking for him? Was it because he was printing those pamphlets? Politics in Yiddish?"

"It must be," said Adela. "And I wouldn't go around asking people so directly, if I were you."

Sorel felt her cheeks flame in response. She wanted Adela to like her, but she felt clumsy and foolish. She wished someone would say the blessing over bread so she could distract herself with breakfast.

"I'm sorry to ask," said Sam, "But what did the men want with you, in particular? Why ask you where Isser was? You're a village cheese-girl."

Adela shot him a hateful look. Sorel looked down to hide a grin: she wasn't the only one annoyed by Sam after all.

"I'm only asking because they told this Isser they were looking for you again," said Sam, unbothered. He added more quietly, "And because I hoped I could find more of the pamphlets. I've sold nearly all of them. The young people in all the villages want to read them."

Adela picked up a bread roll and started to tear it to pieces. She seemed to be turning something over in her head. Sorel took the excuse to start eating herself, though she still felt a bit like a naughty child.

"We ought not to have secrets," said Sam. "You, Adela, you're the only one of us who hasn't admitted any crimes."

"I haven't admitted any crimes!" Sorel objected, mouth full.

"Well, all right—admitted any crimes or been guilty of looking like someone whose crimes it seems the goyim are aware of. He was nearly killed by some men who thought he was your Isser, did he say?"

"He said," said Adela. Then she looked at Sorel, blinked, and shook her head as if to clear it. "But I didn't really hear it. I am sorry we put you in danger."

Sorel mumbled a demurral.

"I don't want to sit here and wait for someone to find me," Adela said. "And you're right, you've put yourselves in danger again, coming here. Alright, I'll show you my secret, then."

She gestured for them to wait as she went out of the room, returning with a sewing box of pretty, carved wood. She lifted out a tray of notions, then a stack of folded cloths, then by a couple of threads she lifted a false bottom from the box and took out a stack of pages in handwritten Yiddish. She placed the pages on the table by Sam's elbow. At a glance, Sorel saw the words *emancipation* and *organization*.

"I'm the translator," Adela said. "No one knows it but Isser. Not even the other printers know. He'd come every few weeks to collect new translations and bring me books."

"You mean no one knows, unless someone got it out of him somehow," said Sam.

"It sounded to me like they just thought you were sweethearts," said Sorel, unsure of whether she wanted to reassure Adela or defend Isser's secret-keeping.

"Either way." Adela packed her sewing box up again, hiding the pages at the bottom. "It doesn't matter what they know about me. What matters is that they don't find out anything more, and that means we have to find Isser. Here's what we'll do. Stay here for the night. My family will be back soon. Papa will be at shul most of the day tomorrow, so he won't notice if

I leave in the morning—you don't mind walking back to Esrog on Shabbat?"

She addressed it to Sorel with a sharp look. Sorel shook her head, not because she had any thoughts about walking on Shabbat, but because Adela's tone demanded agreement. Sam looked uncomfortable but said nothing.

"Good." Adela nodded sharply. "The bathhouse is on the edge of town to the northeast. You'll see the big pines. It's at the edge of the woods there."

Sam got up from the table as if he fully understood this change of subject. Sorel sat a moment longer, confused, but he took her by the elbow and led her out.

"Where are we going?" she asked when they were back in the street.

"I don't know about you, Isser-Alter," he said, "but I am going to the bathhouse. It's erev shabbes, and I've been sleeping on the ground."

Sorel glanced back toward Adela's house. She still didn't understand why they were leaving. Were they not to stay as guests?

Then she remembered she was a boy. Adela's father had only daughters, hadn't someone said so? Of course she couldn't have boys for guests.

Sam was chattering on about baths, but Sorel dragged her feet. She couldn't exactly take a bath with him: he'd find out her secret. She did want to wash off the dirt and some of the horse smell that still clung to her stolen clothes. But she'd have to do it later. Maybe while the men were praying. She didn't think anyone would be using it then.

"I'm tired," she said. "I'm going back to the shul."

"All right," said Sam, unconcerned. "Rest, then. We have more walking tomorrow, sinners that we are."

The Kuritsev shul was neat and cozy inside. Sorel thought it would be stuffy in the summertime, especially in the little alcove that served as a women's gallery. There, she tucked herself behind a bench and curled up with her head on her satchel and her boots off, resting her aching feet. The size of the space and the dust on the floor suggested the women prayed somewhere else, and she didn't expect to be disturbed there. It hadn't been a lie that she was tired. In fact, now that she'd stopped, she wondered how she would ever manage to start walking again. Every part of her ached.

You're spoiled, said the little voice in her head that was a bit too honest.

"Not anymore," she said, out loud, to shut it up. Her breath stirred the dust that hung in the still air behind the screen separating the women's section from the rest of the synagogue. She watched the particles dance in silence until her eyes drifted shut, and she was asleep.

CHAPTER

5

SHE'D THOUGHT the sound of the evening service would wake her. Instead, she opened her eyes to moonlight, bright through the high windows, and the faint cracks of wood settling the way it does in an empty building after everyone has left. She was unspeakably thirsty and her back ached. She hauled herself to her feet, leaning on the wall, and stuck her head out from behind the partition. There was a faint lantern-light by the Holy Ark, and a black shape curled up under a blanket at the edge of the lamplight that she thought was Sam, sleeping. The place was otherwise dark and empty. It must be near midnight, she thought.

She sat back down on the women's bench and fought with herself for a moment over whether she ought to put her shoes back on. Her feet were swollen, but in the end she decided she couldn't cross town in the dark on her bare, tender soles. She picked up the boots and took them with her as she crept out of the synagogue, holding her breath in fear of waking Sam.

She stopped on the front step and pulled her boots on in the light of the bright moon. The square seemed larger now that it was empty, everything silvered in the moonlight. It took her a moment to remember the way to the bathhouse, but once she did, there was a sense of freedom in walking by herself. No need to rush and no need to hide with everyone tucked away for the night. Kuritsev smelled clean and fresh, with faint traces of roast chicken and challah in the air that made her stomach growl. She had not anticipated how hungry all this walking would make her. She wished she'd eaten more at Adela's house, that she hadn't felt the awkwardness of being the only one to reach for the food. She pressed a hand to her belly and silently told it to be quiet.

The bathhouse was at the very edge of the village, next to a running brook that seemed to supply the drinking water and power a mill downstream, if she understood what she was seeing in the dark. She worried there might be an attendant, sleeping by the stove perhaps, but when she cautiously pushed open the door, there was only a damp heat. The lingering embers of the fire still warmed the air. She blocked the door behind her with a wedge of firewood and stripped out of her clothes, shaking them out to try to remove some of the dust of the road.

She sat on a stool and scrubbed herself with a cake of herb-scented soap in water that had gone cold. She would have minded more if it wasn't such a relief to no longer be grimy. She washed herself twice just for the pleasure of being clean, then crossed to the little alcove that held the mikveh and slipped into the water. Here it was cold as ice. She gasped before her head went under, but the cold pulled the ache from her bones and brushed the wisps of fatigue out of her mind. She hung suspended in the water, holding her breath, until she could no longer stand it.

When she pulled herself up on the lip of the pool, she heard music. At first, she thought it was the ringing of water in her ears. After pushing the hair back from her face and shaking her head to clear her eyes, the sound clearly remained. She recognized the chime of bridle bells mixed with the wailing of a fiddle and the sweet high crying of a flute. Something about it made her shiver more than the icy water had.

She hauled herself out of the water, squeezing her hair—a whisper of some nursemaid in the back of her head telling her not to squeeze water from a cloth on the sabbath, which she ignored—and took a cloth from the stack by the soap in the bathing room to dry herself quickly. She dressed in a hurry and kicked the wedge out from under the door.

There was a parade of people outside the bathhouse. What had been an empty road, passing the bathhouse and the mill on its way to the woods or to nowhere, grey earth under the moon, was now lit golden with lanterns and crowded as a Saint's day at market. Sorel stood baffled in the doorway, trying to understand what she saw. The road was packed with people in their finest clothes, carrying instruments or lanterns or waving bouquets of flowers, light glinting off gold threads of embroidery and sparkling in their dark eyes. A gaggle of children with the clawed feet of owls ran past her, shrieking with laughter, their mouths full of fangs like cats, and she rubbed her eyes. Back toward the town square, a lady on a shining white horse tossed coins into the crowd.

Enchanted, Sorel stepped out of the bathhouse and caught at the sleeve of a passing young woman. "What is this? Who are you?"

The girl laughed and didn't answer. "Come dance with us!"

She caught Sorel by the hand and drew her into the procession. They were all following the lady in white, the crowd singing in a cacophony of languages, none of which Sorel could understand. The girl who'd caught her spun her round and round, until she was dizzy and stumbling, then drew her close to whisper in her ear.

"Who are you, little prince?"

"Isser-Alter!" someone shouted from behind her, and she felt a tug on her collar. When she turned, there was the boy from her dream—only he wasn't wearing her face this time. As himself, he was shorter than she was, with darker hair and deep, bruised shadows under his eyes, but she knew he was the same person.

"Isser," she repeated numbly. She wanted to go back to the dancing. The girl's hair was a spill of ink over her shoulders, the lantern light casting shadows beneath her collarbones and painting her lips a bright, wine red. She pouted at the two of them and held out her other hand to the newcomer.

"Dance with me," she said.

"No," he said, and pulled Sorel away. "We have to talk, please listen to me."

Sorel tried to follow the girl into the crowd, but lost her, the boy holding her tight by the collar. She tried to brush him off, and the touch of his skin on hers burned like ice.

"Sorel," he whispered. "Don't tell them your name."

Her head was foggy, as though she'd been drinking wine. She thought she knew him, but she couldn't remember his name.

"You shouldn't let Adela go back to Esrog," he said, in the same urgent whisper. "Please, stop her."

This, Sorel understood. With a twinge of resentment at his presumption, she said, "I'll let Adela do whatever she likes."

"You can't," he said desperately. "You have to tell her it's too dangerous!"

"She knows it's dangerous. I'm done doing the sensible thing and I'm not going to make anyone else do it, either."

"It's not the same," he said. "And you shouldn't be going back there, either. You owe me. I helped you run."

That was where she knew him from—his voice. The voice of her yetzer hara, that told her to take the first step, the leap out her window.

"It's you, isn't it," she said. "Isser. The real one."

"Don't go back to Esrog," he said. "Don't be so foolish. You have to look for my body."

"Your body? Where?"

He looked exasperated. "I don't know; I'm not with it, am I."

"Then how—" Sorel began to say, but the girl with the red lips was back, hanging on her arm, offering her wine.

"Come with me," she said. "Come and see the queen! She'll want to see you."

Sorel blinked at her and then looked back at Isser, already forgetting what they'd been talking about. He seemed to be standing in darkness, even in the pool of light from the lanterns, as if only he were still lit by moonlight alone, his eyes great black pools of shadow.

The girl was drawing her away.

"Check in your pocket!" Isser shouted after them. "Your pocket, Isser-Alter!"

Confused, Sorel put her hands in her pockets, and gasped as something sliced her fingers, sharp as a razor blade. She pulled her hand out to check if her fingers were bleeding, and as she did, she heard a burst of sound, deep ferocious barking that shook her to the bone. A cold wind blasted down the street, making her cover her head, and when she looked up again, she was standing alone on the dirt road in the darkness.

No one was there.

The dog growled, low, in the shadows. She turned and found it standing between her and the path back to the bathhouse, its massive shoulders hunched, teeth bared and shining.

Someone had told her once never to run from a growling dog.

The advice was no use to her now—she turned and ran, expecting at every second to be knocked to the ground, expecting the bite of its jaws on her neck. She ran flat-out back to the synagogue, shoved a bench against the door, and collapsed, gasping, onto the floor.

SAM WOKE HER to the pink of early morning, tapping her on the shoulder.

"They'll be coming soon for shacharis," he said. "We're meant to meet Adela."

The bench was no longer wedged in front of the door. Sorel looked, and thought she saw scuff marks on the floorboards where she'd dragged it, but maybe it was her imagination. Maybe she'd been dreaming. Surely she must have been—she could think of no other explanation for the parade of lanterns, the black dog that hadn't killed her, or even why Sam wouldn't have woken at her noisy, panicked return.

"Find my body" Isser had said. Isser, her other self. She could almost feel him, hovering just over her shoulder like a worried attendant.

"Adela," she said, and shoved herself upright. Isser had told her to keep Adela out of danger, but she didn't see the sense in it. Wasn't Adela in danger anyway? Why not face it head on? And anyway, how could she find anything of Isser's without Adela's help?

"I always feel I've slept so well, when it's a shul," said Sam conversationally, as they went out into the square. "Don't you?"

"Not really," said Sorel. She was still trying to sort the reality of the night from the dream. Her hair was clean, the sweat and dust gone from her skin, so she must really have gone to the bathhouse. Maybe she dozed off on her feet while walking back.

Adela was waiting for them at the edge of the village, sitting on a fence with her braids tucked into a man's hat and eating a raisin bun. She had more buns in a satchel and handed one each to Sam and Sorel as they said good morning. Sorel ate hers in three bites, still starving, and Sam, watching her askance, handed his to her.

"You're too skinny, anyway," he said.

"I haven't been on the road so long," Sorel said, defensive. "I'm not used to so much walking."

"Well, there's more of it," said Adela. "I have a contact in Esrog to talk to. He won't be in shul; we can catch him. A friend," she added, at Sam's skeptical look. "We've known him forever. Isser and I attended the Russian schools with him."

CHAPTER

6

SOREL EXPECTED ADELA to bring them back to the print shop, or somewhere near it, but she brought them instead to a street by the river, almost *in* the river. The ground underfoot was spongy and a creeping moss or algae grew up the walls of the run-down houses. The bank sloped so steeply down to the river that the next street up was nearly at the height of the roofs. The pitch gave everything a cramped aspect, as if they were half in a cave. It was hard to imagine that anyone living here would have any books, much less books to translate; Sorel couldn't help thinking they would turn to mold as quickly as soft bread. The children who played in the street mostly wore no shoes, and the dogs and goats who picked through the piles of trash in the corners looked both skinny and swollen, their coats dull.

Sorel had never been in a neighborhood like this before; it was not appropriate for someone like herself—the daughter of Kalman the lumber merchant, distantly related to the Vilna Gaon himself, and engaged to the Esroger Rebbe's own son—to be seen anywhere so depressed and dirty. Her father would have been horrified, which in turn delighted Sorel. She imagined him at home in his study, clutching his heart with a spasm of dismay—and then remembered that he was probably searching for her, and might even be in Esrog himself, which made her all the gladder that he wouldn't think of finding her in a place like this.

Adela seemed to have no hesitation for her own sake and marched ahead in her farmer's boots without bothering to avoid the puddles. Sorel tried to emulate the disregard for the mud, thinking her own instinct to pick her way around by the driest path might remind people that this was not her natural place. She could feel Sam's eyes on her nearly all the time. Though every time she turned to glare at him, he was looking elsewhere.

Adela stopped at a tavern that was barely more than a shopfront with a pair of old men leaning their elbows on an upturned pickle barrel. Sorel couldn't tell if the place was open for business in defiance of Shabbat, or if it simply didn't have a door to close to keep the alter-kackers out. When they stopped, a scrawny spotted dog jumped to its feet in the doorway and barked at them, but Sam glared at it and it turned away, chagrined, and slunk into the unlit interior.

"Where's Yoshke?" Adela asked the oldsters.

The pair had what looked like an entire silent conversation between themselves, looking from Adela to each other and back with a few cursory glances at Sorel and Sam. Then one said, "Nice girl like you doesn't want to know where Yoshke is."

"I do," said Adela. She folded her arms and planted her boots, looking to Sorel as if a team of oxen couldn't budge her. "You know why I want to know? He owes me money."

One of the men laughed a sort of helpless laugh. "You and half the Jewish street."

"And none of you have the kishkes to go get it from him?" said Adela. "It takes a little girl to do it?"

The other old man looked uncomfortable, and turned his face to Sorel, as if seeking help. "You shouldn't let her run around like this."

"Me?" said Sorel, astonished. "What have I got to do with it?"

"We're also looking for Yoshke," Sam interrupted, so close at Sorel's elbow that she jumped. "He owes you money, does he, grandfather?"

"He might, if it weren't the sabbath," said the uncomfortable old man, shifting in his seat. "This isn't appropriate."

"If it weren't the sabbath, would you want that money back, in exchange for telling us where to find him?" said Adela.

"You two boys," said the other old man, gesturing at Sorel and Sam. "Two strong lads, we can tell. A girl? The wives would see us skinned."

This made Sorel remember she was a boy. That was why the old man wanted her to stop Adela from talking—just like Isser had asked. See who's on your side? She thought at him, deliberately. His voice in her head stayed silent, but she couldn't tell if it was because he saw the point or he simply wasn't there.

"There's a spot on the bank down that way," the more helpful of the elders was saying now. "He's got a boat; he rows people across to the forest or the beys oylem for a fee. If he does anything else I don't know about it."

"Even this much we didn't hear from you," Sam promised. "Gut shabbes."

The old men returned his gut shabbes with guilty looks, as if they weren't quite sure why they were bothering. Adela started walking again without giving a farewell, and Sorel jogged to catch up.

"Who's Yoshke? Why shouldn't a nice girl go to see him?"

Adela turned a fierce look in her direction, and she felt her cheeks heat up.

"I don't even think you are a nice girl," she defended herself.

Adela laughed, a single sharp bark.

"I just want to know what to expect," said Sorel. She desperately wanted to hide her face. What was she saying?

"I told you, I know him from the Russian schools," said Adela. "But more important—he's a smuggler. And an all-around scoundrel. That's why no one should want to talk to him, but he'll know where to find Isser if no one else does."

Sorel hadn't gone to the Russian school—the secular schools had a poor reputation and taught barely anything Jewish. Respectable girls like herself wouldn't go because there were boys there, and respectable boys wouldn't go because they needed to learn Talmud instead. Only the poorer Jews, who couldn't bribe their way out of the state obligation, attended. She was a little surprised Adela would have been allowed but didn't want to ask about it so soon after her other blunder. If she seemed too interested in women's matters, she was afraid Adela would see through her. Men she trusted not to notice anything odd, but women were different. Women looked each other in the face.

"Be on the lookout," Adela added. "Yoshke I don't trust, but I know his tricks. His friends, I might not know—if he has any."

"Right," said Sorel. She checked over her shoulder, as if Yoshke's unsavory friends might be behind her, or some other danger like the black dog from the alley—but there was only Sam, tilting an eyebrow at her as if they were sharing a joke.

"He looks like muscle," Adela acknowledged, as if Sorel had been looking to him on purpose. "You, not so much, but at least you're tall."

"I have a knife," Sorel added. "I've stabbed a man with it already; I'd do it again."

Adela gave her an odd look, and she realized it hadn't been a civilized thing to say. On the other hand, Adela didn't look entirely put off by it.

"God forbid you have to," Adela said after a moment's thought.

YOSHKE'S BOATHOUSE was at the end of an alley so low on the riverbank that every step brought water out of the earth under-foot. Here Sorel smelled no Shabbat feasting aromas, only the cool living odor of damp. She thought once or twice she saw someone watching them from inside one of the ramshackle houses, but it seemed everyone kept to themselves here. She wrapped her hand around the hilt of the knife in her pocket and flinched for a moment at a memory of the cold biting her fingers last night, before the dog appeared.

You can always run again, said Isser in her head, *but if you run, you have to take Adela with you.*

YOSHKE WAS UNMISTAKABLE. Everyone else in this neighbor-hood looked washed-out, downtrodden, and shifty. The young man lounging on a herring box in front of the little boathouse looked like he belonged to a different neighborhood entirely. He was dressed in the modern style, with his hair slicked back and a carefully trimmed little mustache. Sorel wondered how he had managed to get here without dirtying his shiny leather shoes. He was smoking a cigarette, and evidently spent a good deal of time lounging by the boathouse smoking them, as little scraps of burnt paper littered the ground beneath his seat.

"Adela," he said, in the manner of a gracious host. "What the devil brings you here?"

"What do you think? I'm looking for Isser."

"Not so much as a good shabbes," said Yoshke, pretending to be wounded. He looked over her shoulders at Sorel and Sam. "Who are these people?"

"Friends," said Adela. "Is there somewhere we can talk?"

"Friends who know Isser's business?" said Yoshke.

Adela huffed impatiently. "I wouldn't bring them otherwise. Don't waste my time, Yoshke. I walked here from Kuritsev, and my feet hurt."

"Well, all right." Yoshke heaved himself up as if it were a terrible imposition. "I know where there's a peasant who'll sell you lunch on shabbes and not tell the hasids. Come on."

Sorel watched his feet as they walked and realized he kept his shoes shiny by picking his way between the puddles like a cat. Watching it made her feel ridiculous for having wanted to do the same, and she stepped in one puddle on purpose out of spite before realizing that her felt boots weren't waterproof.

Her stomach had woken up at the mention of food, and she realized she was once again starving. She'd never needed to eat so much in her life.

Yoshke's peasant had a little tavern up the hill, which smelled strongly of spilled ale and tobacco. It was a mix of Jews and gentiles, but only men. Yoshke offered Adela a seat on a bench with a gentlemanly flourish that made Sorel want to stomp on his patent-leather toes. The peasant brought them bowls of something brown and spicy that Sorel was certain was not kosher. Sam turned up his nose at it, pushing his bowl in her direction, as she shoveled the stew into her mouth without any concern over what kinds of unclean animals had given their lives to make it. It tasted good, even if it were only hunger that told her so.

"How's the family?" Yoshke said to Adela, after devouring his own bowl with unseemly haste. "Your sisters are healthy? Is Hasia married yet?"

"None of your business," said Adela. "They're all healthy. Where's Isser? When did you see him last?"

"I don't know," said Yoshke. "Three, four days? A week? Two? I'm not his mother."

Sorel could tell Adela was trying to be diplomatic, but she had no patience for it. "You work with him, don't you? If you work with him, you should care where he is, because there are men looking for him who'll kill you if you don't have an answer."

Yoshke looked at her askance.

"I don't mean us," she said, gesturing to herself and Sam. "But I could mean us, if you don't start talking. Have those goyim been after you to find Isser, or not?"

"No, no, no," said Yoshke. "No goyim, nothing like that—I don't even really work with him, all right? He's made a stamp for me maybe. One or two times, that's all, just a little job. I don't get into all that political stuff; it's too complicated, all that intellectual business." He was looking at Adela now. "That's not my field. I don't like it and I don't trust it. So no, I don't know where Isser is. Maybe you should ask that weaselly little hasid."

"What weaselly little hasid?" said Adela, frowning.

"Why should I know the names of all Isser's friends? The hasid who looks like a weasel! I don't know. I saw them sometimes in the beys oylem."

"Doing what?" said Sorel. All these poor Jews spent so much time in the cemetery! As if it were a public park.

"Talking, I assume," said Yoshke. "Perhaps about books— God knows it's hard to get Isser to talk about anything else."

"When was this?" Adela asked. "Did it happen often?"

"Mainly Sundays," said Yoshke. "Not that I kept track, mind you. I don't care what Isser does with his time. Only the other one used my boat sometimes."

"What did he look like?" said Sorel. "And don't say weasel again, we all heard that already."

"Jewish," said Yoshke, unhelpfully. "Listen, I'm a professional. I don't go around sharing anyone's business but my own, and if Isser's in trouble I don't want to be mixed up in it, all right? And neither should a young lady."

"There aren't any young ladies here," said Sorel, forgetting Adela for a moment. "What do you mean Isser made you a stamp?"

Yoshke made a shushing gesture, looking around the tavern as if someone might have overheard. "Don't just go flapping your jaws in public! Who are you, anyway? What grave did Adela dig you out of?"

"He's from down the river," said Sam, smoothly covering for Sorel as if he'd known her forever. "We've all been in business with Isser. I sell his pamphlets. So none of us need to have secrets."

"Not that big of a secret, anyway," said Adela in an undertone. "The whole riverbank district knows what Yoshke sells. It's a customs stamp, Alter—to show the tax has been paid on goods from Romania."

This Sorel understood. It was a constant aggravation to her father that the gentiles believed Jewish smugglers were responsible for bringing things from Romania untaxed—liquor, cloth, sweets, anything worth having. He was always trying to convince the gentile officials that to the contrary of their expectations, Jews were honest dealers. He mainly seemed to demonstrate his honesty by bribing them, but he was never happy about it. She'd assumed that perpetual thorn in his side, the Jewish smuggler from Esrog, was a sort of phantom. Yet here she sat looking at one.

"It doesn't matter what the whole riverbank knows, it's still no good tempting the evil eye," said Yoshke. "This is why you and Isser are bashert, Adela, because neither of you knows when to keep your mouth shut and your eyes on your own work."

"My mouth has been shut," Adela said, "but it doesn't have to stay that way. What do you suppose would happen if we went to the rebbe or to the kehillah and tell them what you've been doing? The gentiles will work with you as long as you're turning them a profit, but they'll never work with you again if we make your name public."

Yoshke's eyes darted around the room. Sorel remembered that Adela had described him as a friend, and suddenly wondered what sort of friendships ordinary people had. She'd never had any friends herself, but she'd read about them in books, and this was not how they tended to look.

"If you don't know where Isser is, show us someone who will know," said Adela. "Get us a meeting with Pavlikov."

Yoshke looked from her to Sam, who was simply gazing steadily back at him, to Sorel, who showed him the handle of her knife, for encouragement. He sighed and slumped in his seat.

"Pavlikov," he grumbled. "Fine, fine. If you're determined to tempt the Angel of Death, who am I to stop you?"

CHAPTER

7

ISSER KNEW the shortest way from his own rooms to Yoshke's boathouse like the back of his hand, but with the rebbe's stolen book tucked into his vest, he felt as if he were being watched at every step. Each dark window became an eye, each overhanging eave a reaching hand, and the shadows cast by his lantern leapt at his back like great black dogs. He cursed himself for letting Ostap have his knife; the cold, sinister weight of it would have reassured him. His heart was pounding by the time he reached the river-bottom district, and he'd never been so relieved to see Yoshke, sitting on a fish crate and smoking outside his shed.

"How goes it?" Yoshke said, gesturing Isser to sit on the other crate beside him. Isser sat, out of breath and trying to hide it. The sense of something chasing him had only gotten

stronger the closer he got to the river, and his head was full
of the heady spiced perfume of the book, drowning out even
the familiar damp smell of the lower streets.

"How's business?" he asked, hoping to brush off Yoshke's
question, but Yoshke was giving him a strange look.

"You look like you've got a dybbuk on you," Yoshke said.
"If you're in trouble you'd damn well better not have brought
it to me."

"Thanks a lot for the concern, brother," Isser grumbled, and
took a deliberate deep breath. There was no one chasing him;
the alleys were empty, as they should be this time of night,
and the only sounds were the distant chatter of voices at the
tavern a few streets over and the constant rush of the river.
Yoshke himself was no danger. Isser didn't trust him, exactly,
but he knew how not to trust him.

"I'm looking for a trip across the river," he said. "I know
it's not your regular time, but I'll pay for it."

"Are you fleeing the city?" Yoshke asked, a little too loudly.
Isser shushed him, and he leaned in, resting his hand on
Isser's shoulder so that the cigarette between his fingers
wrapped them both in smoke. He repeated the question, in
a whisper.

"I'm not fleeing the city. I just need you to take me across
and wait—maybe half an hour—and take me back."

Yoshke inspected his face closely, as if he could read Isser's mind by looking at him for long enough. At last, he sat

back and knocked the ash off his cigarette on the side of his boot. "What for? That's part of the payment."

"Asking questions is not part of your business," Isser objected. "Asking questions isn't part of anyone's business."

"It's my business when you keep twitching like you're sitting on hot coals," said Yoshke. "What is it? The city guards are after you for selling political rags? The kahal found out you're telling their wives to stop paying the kosher meat tax and take their wigs off? Or Pavlikov found out you know about the guns—is that it?"

"I don't care about Pavlikov's damn guns," said Isser. "Shut up, would you?"

"No one's listening," Yoshke hissed, leaning closer again regardless. "You know you can't hear a damn thing two steps from here. You can't lie to me, brother. Something's happened."

Isser sighed. It would do no good to sit here fighting until the sun came up. "All right, fine. Swear on your mother that you'll keep it a secret."

"Swear on my damn mother," said Yoshke. "And your mother too, may she rest in peace."

"I'm doing a job," said Isser. "For Kalman Senderovich. Only not the usual—getting him uncensored books or whatever. He asked me to steal something from the rebbe."

"From the rebbe? Didn't they just announce they've engaged his daughter to that little friend of yours, that weasel?"

"Right."

"So what's he doing stealing from his own daughter's father-in-law?"

"Exactly my question," said Isser.

"So you've stolen something from the rebbe," said Yoshke, "and now your little shtetl-peasant ass is scared he's put a curse on you, is that it? Have you ever actually seen him do a miracle? He never has. Not since we've been alive, not once. If he could perform miracles we wouldn't have half as much cholera. You need to stop talking to women."

"I'm not afraid I'm cursed," Isser snapped, although truth be told he was, a bit. "I'm afraid he's going to send someone after me with a real-life, modern, solid cudgel—or a gun, for that matter. You think the rebbe can't get what Pavlikov can? They buy from the same sellers."

He waved his hand through the space between them, indicating Yoshke and himself—not that Isser had ever sold anyone a weapon, but he'd certainly sold equally incriminating literature to Pavlikov, the connoisseur of European politics; and the rebbe, whose taste ran to illegal Hasidic mysticism.

Yoshke laughed. "I'd like to see the rebbe with a gun. I'd love to see him try to shoot you, actually. In a duel, like Russian noblemen do."

"I wouldn't," said Isser. "Are you going to take me across to the cemetery or not? I have a meeting to get to."

"I'll take you," said Yoshke. "But if Kalman Senderovich takes what you stole and buries you in the woods so you can't tell his secrets, I won't go looking for your body. And the price is double, for making me the rebbe's enemy."

Isser dug in his pocket for the coins. It wasn't as if he could just swim.

OLD RUKHELE, as expected, was sitting by her little fire in the cemetery, knitting something shapeless out of dark wool. Isser wasn't sure she ever slept. She said it was because she was old, but he thought there was more to it. The same restlessness that made her insist on sleeping outside the city, maybe, and not taking charity from the kahal.

When Isser came through the cemetery gate she turned her head toward him, face lifted like a hound scenting the air. Something about the movement made him stop in his tracks, feeling caught, even though she was the one he'd been looking for to start with.

"Israel," she said, her rich, deep voice as startling as always. "What have you brought me?"

"Brought you?" He felt his hand go involuntarily to his vest pocket, the disguised angelic book. She couldn't know. But he had the sense that she'd smelled it, somehow. The perfume couldn't possibly be that strong. The wind wasn't even in the right direction. It was his imagination—Kalman Senderovich and the rebbe had him dybbuk-ridden, like Yoshke said. "I've brought you a question."

"A question," said Rukhele. "That's even better than a meal. What is it?"

Isser sat himself on her side of the fire. He would have liked to keep everything secret, ask no one for help, and keep them all out of it. But whatever wedge this book drove between Kalman and the rebbe, Isser wanted to control it. And to control it, he had to understand it.

"You know a lot about certain things," he started, hesitant. "Cures, and fortune-telling, and so forth. Do you know anything about angels?"

"You'll have to be much, much more specific," said Old Rukhele, flashing him a grin.

"If, say, someone had a book that purported to be written by an angel," said Isser. He hardly knew what order to explain things in. It was all so ridiculous, so petty—unless it was real. And if it were real, it was so far beyond his understanding. "What advice would you give that person?"

"Akh, zunenyu," said Rukhele. "I'd say you're already in over your head, and whatever you did to get there, God forbid, it would have been better not to do it. The rebbe's book, is it?"

Isser's hand went to his vest again. She must have heard the movement, and known what it meant—she nodded, solemn.

"I think you've done a dangerous thing, bringing that outside the eruv," she said. "They say the Angels of Death wrote that book with their own hands on behalf of the first Esroger Rebbe, and anyone who handles it, Death knows their name."

"What does the eruv have to do with it?" Isser asked, glancing over his shoulder, toward Yoshke and the river and the city walls.

"It's said the rebbe—the first rebbe—made a bargain with the Angel of Death to avert a plague upon the Jews of Esrog hundreds of years ago. Since then as long as the Esroger Rebbe holds court in his shtibl whatever disasters come to the outside world can't touch us, and the angel can't come to the city. But if the book that binds the angel were to be removed . . ." She trailed off and cocked her head at him, smiling crookedly. "It's a nice fairytale, isn't it?"

"The Angel of Death visits Esrog all the time," said Isser, confused. "I mean, people die here. My mother, God rest her, had the cholera, for heaven's sake."

"That's true," said Rukhele. "So it must be a story only."

"If the book gives the rebbe power somehow, if it's meant to protect the Jewish community," said Isser, "then—"

He stopped. He'd been about to tell her that he'd taken it on the word of Kalman Senderovich. What did Kalman want with it?

"The book was meant as a contract of sorts," said Rukhele. "Or that was the story, anyway. My man used to tell it. He was born here, you know, before he was set to wandering, may he rest in peace. He died, well—you must have been very young, then. The river took him, poor thing. He said that the one who holds the book may speak to the angel, and so the greedy might want it, thinking to gain power. But speaking to an angel is like standing on the edge of a waterfall. Any little slip, and there will be nothing left of you."

CHAPTER

8

PAVLIKOV, THE GENTILE SMUGGLER, could be found in a tavern called the Hound's Head, but only after dark. He slept during the day, like a vampire. They would have to wait to talk to him. In the meantime Yoshke needed to make arrangements and couldn't have Sorel and her friends tagging after him like ducklings. To get rid of them, he sent them to the Gravediggers' Synagogue, in a nearby courtyard, which was a slumped and crooked little building with a set of steep stairs leading to a women's gallery that Yoshke promised would be entirely empty and a fine place for hiding. Sorel got the sense that he knew from experience and wondered what sorts of insidious business she'd missed by only ever attending shul when she had to.

The Gravediggers' Synagogue smelled of damp earth, as if the work of those who'd funded its construction had followed them to their services. No one was there except for a little old man who sat on an armchair by the Ark, fast asleep. Adela started up the stairs to the women's gallery and stopped when she realized Sorel wasn't following.

"There won't be any women up there, you know," she said sardonically. "They're all at home, serving the second meal."

"Right," said Sorel. She made herself take a step forward, ignoring the little anxious instinct that suggested an angel might strike the veils from her companions' eyes as soon as they saw her in a feminine context. Although there was hardly anything identifiably feminine about the little gallery. It was quite dark, being above the lamps that hung on the walls of the men's section, and there were a few boxes stacked up against the wall as if the gallery were used for storage. Sam curled up on a bench and went immediately to sleep, leaving Sorel and Adela sitting as comfortably as they could in the cramped space, Adela leafing idly through a Yiddish prayerbook.

"You went to a secular school?" Sorel asked, when the silence got too awkward for her. "A Russian school?"

She stopped herself before adding with boys? Because she was quite sure Adela would laugh at that.

"That's right," said Adela. "My mother saw that I liked reading, so I'd be the one to make the most of it. She was distantly related to the famous Genius of Vilna, my mother."

"We're related, then," said Sorel. "So is my father. But he never sent me to any goyish school."

Adela looked her over. "You've got clean hands. Your father is rich?"

Sorel felt her cheeks warming. What else could be seen so clearly? "He is. But I ran away from him."

"And your mother?"

"Dead, may she rest in peace."

"You learned Hebrew?" Adela asked.

"Some," said Sorel, feeling cagy. She knew plenty of boys suffered through years of cheder without really learning anything, but she still felt self-conscious about her lack of mishnah. She'd learned German instead. But Isser knew German, didn't he? She'd seen German books in his room. "Isser went to the school with you?"

"That hasid Yoshke mentioned," Adela said, frowning into the distance. "I wonder if it's him—there was a hasid's son, a wealthy one, and they paid for Isser to be sent in his place, so the goyish learning wouldn't poison him. If I could remember his name, we could find him. I think I'd recognize him if I saw him. If this Pavlikov doesn't know anything, we can try at the rebbe's court."

"I don't think you'll find out much there," said Sorel. "They don't like talking to women."

Adela rolled her eyes. "I am aware of that, thank you, Alter."

"Right. Just, they'll really notice you."

"That's why I said if Pavlikov doesn't know anything."

Adela's exasperation made Sorel shut her mouth. She wished Isser would whisper advice in her ear for talking to Adela, but he was nowhere to be found. The presence she'd felt early in the morning was gone now. He could at least have saved her from looking foolish in front of his friend.

Discouraged, she picked up another of the Yiddish prayer books and pretended she was reading.

THE SUN WAS ANGLED LOW and all three of them were dozing when Sam suddenly sat up, startling Sorel.

"What is it?" she asked. He had a look on his face like he'd heard some kind of alarm, but she couldn't hear anything.

"Something's happening in the street," he said, getting up. Adela put her book away and followed him to the stairs, where they both paused to listen. Sorel, feeling left out, went to the window and looked out to see that there was indeed something happening in the street: a gaggle of men in black coats were having what looked like a heated discussion while a few children and women hung by, the way people always did when there was a story to collect.

"We'd better see," said Adela, already starting down the stairs. Sorel checked that her knife was in her pocket and followed.

On the steps of the shul, Sam was already asking what had happened.

"They found someone in the river!" said a cheder-age child in bare feet.

"Not someone," corrected his companion with shoes but no hat. "They found something."

One of the women spoke up. "It's a murder!"

"No, no, no. It's only that it could be a murder."

"Who actually saw what happened?" said Sam, cutting through the discussion. Everyone pointed. In the center of the flock of black coats, there was a peasant holding something sodden. If you glanced briefly, you might have thought it was a body, albeit a small one.

Sorel and Adela elbowed their way closer, Sam on their heels. Sorel had forgotten about Isser for the moment. She was trying to get a better look to see if the peasant were holding what she thought he was. It was a heavy bundle of fabric, dark as blood with the river water.

Her wedding dress.

"We have to ask the rebbe," one of the black coats said, at her shoulder. "The rebbe will know if it's permissible to start a search before the end of Shabbat."

"We don't have time! The rebbe isn't even in town. He's at his son's father-in-law's house. If someone is drowned in the river, we have to find them before it's too late."

The argument was going in circles.

Sam said, "Could you ask the gentiles to search the river instead?"

All of this conversation was going on in Yiddish. The peasant holding the gown looked very lost. Sorel moved closer to him, heart pounding in her mouth, and spoke to him in Russian. "What is that you've found?"

"It's a girl's dress," he said. "I thought it looked like it would be a Jewess, so I brought it here—I was looking for Mendel the gravedigger, I know him; he goes to this synagogue and he's the only Jew I know."

He shook out the gown to show her and she flinched away from it, involuntarily. It looked so heavy.

"Isn't it a wedding dress?" someone said in Yiddish.

Someone else was saying, in Sorel's other ear, "If it's a Jewish girl that's drowned, we can't leave her for the goyim to find."

"But if it's a Christian girl it can't be us that finds her! Things are bad enough already! Didn't you hear there were gentile men found murdered behind the Great Synagogue the other day? Torn to pieces by a werewolf!"

"So? Who ever heard of a Jewish werewolf? And it can't have anything to do with this."

Sorel was becoming exasperated and also wanted to get away from this crowd before anyone noticed she and the dress were sized for one another. She grabbed it out of the peasant's hand and turned over the collar. "It's a Jewish girl's dress, you meshuggeners!" she shouted. "Look, someone's sewn a bracha in it."

Immediately everyone needed to take a look at her nurse's careful needlework. The patch with the bracha, which Sorel had found so embarrassing when she first saw it, its evidence of arthritic fingers' wasted efforts—now it seemed to shine with inner light, as if it were a patch from the gown of the Sabbath Queen herself.

"It is a bracha," Sam agreed. The dress was now in his hands: Sorel hadn't even felt him take it amidst all the pushing and shoving. The peasant was looking lost again. "It is a bracha for Soreh bas Kalman."

She hadn't bothered to read it. Why had her nurse put her name? They must be the only words the woman knew in the Holy Language!

Now everyone was talking at once.

"The rebbe's daughter-in-law?"

"But she's supposed to be at her father's house, celebrating her wedding!"

"The rebbe's daughter-in-law has been murdered!"

Sorel grabbed Sam by an elbow and looked around for Adela. The dress had passed back into the hands of the black-coated Hasidim, who, having realized the urgency of a missing girl now that the girl meant something to the rebbe, now wanted to urgently search the river. Adela had gone back to stand on the steps of the shul to escape the crowd, and Sorel dragged Sam over to her.

"It's nothing to do with Isser," she said. "We should get out of here."

"Did they say a girl had gone in the river?" asked Adela.

"That's what they think, anyway," said Sorel. "But no one's seen a girl in the river, so who knows. We need to wait here for Yoshke, don't we? We needn't bother with it."

"It would be terrible luck if something happened to the rebbe's daughter-in-law," said Sam. "God forbid she should be drowned, or anyone drowned."

"It's terrible luck for us if we get involved in any more trouble," said Sorel. They could not go searching for her own body drowned in the river. Someone, eventually, would remember what Kalman's daughter looked like.

"They were looking for a missing girl before," Sam mused. "Weren't they? At the Great Synagogue, weren't the Hasidim looking for a girl?"

"That can't be right," said Sorel shortly. "Not if it's the rebbe's daughter-in-law. She's not missing, she's at her wedding."

Sam was still gazing thoughtfully after the crowd of searchers, who were headed for the river, or else for Mendel the gravedigger's house to get him to talk to his poor baffled peasant friend. The sun had slipped below the rooftops and the group seemed to melt into the shadows of the narrow street.

Sorel jostled Sam by the elbow, drawing his gaze away.

"We are waiting for Yoshke," she said. "Don't get distracted!"

"We should be careful of Yoshke, by the way," said Adela. "I'm not sure I trust him."

Sorel huffed out an irritable breath. "Now she tells us!"

"I just think, keynehore, there is more going on in Esrog than I realized," said Sam.

THE HOUND'S HEAD was uphill in a gentile neighborhood, a part of Esrog Sorel had never been in before. Most of the Jewish neighborhood was run-down, aside from a few streets in the proximity of the Great Synagogue. Conversely most of the gentile neighborhoods were decent, but this was the exception to the rule, a street paved mainly in mud and garbage, with the buildings slumping to one side as if at any moment they might give up and slide down the hill toward the river. The Hound's Head itself could be seen from afar because it had the most lights of any building on the street—most shops had already closed their shutters for the Christian sabbath tomorrow—and there was a spill of men outside it, smoking and talking in loud voices, with a couple of ragged dogs at their feet begging for God knew what.

Yoshke led Sorel, Sam, and Adela around the back to the stable-yard and from there up an outdoor staircase to the second floor. Sorel immediately distrusted the situation. She didn't like not having a readily available exit. When she glanced at Sam, his face indicated that he was thinking on the same lines as her; his hands were half-clenched, halfway to a fist. Adela just looked stubborn and angry.

Yoshke took them down a hallway that stank of tobacco and knocked on the door of a room. "Guests for Mister Pavlikov!" he called out. His Russian was quite good; it was the first real sign of an education Sorel had seen in him.

Someone opened the door and let them into a smoky, brightly lit room that smelled of men and alcohol. Sorel curled her hand around the knife in her pocket and stepped subconsciously closer to Adela. Sam was reassuringly solid at her back.

The room was full of gamblers, a large group around a central table and others crammed around smaller tables in every corner. Nearly everyone was smoking, and they were also drinking and eating pickles and they looked as if they had been doing so for quite some time. Their faces were all red, and some of them looked teary-eyed, either because they were drunk or because they were losing money, probably both. Many of them were wearing shiny cuff links that contrasted with the threadbare fabric of their suits.

Sorel had read as many Russian novels as she could, and so she had images of such places in her head, but the prickle of romance that one felt when Pushkin described it was entirely absent when one was actually standing in the room, being stared at by a bunch of young gentile men in flashy jackets.

At the same time, she felt a prickle of familiarity. She had been somewhere like this before—she was sure of it. But she didn't like it. She had not wanted to be there, she thought. The feeling was fleeting, elusive, like accidentally touching a bruise she hadn't known was there. It was gone as soon as she tried to examine it more closely.

"You didn't tell us you were bringing Queen Esther," said the young man who sat at the head of the large table. He was a bit older than Yoshke or Sorel, in his twenties, but he had the same mustache as Yoshke, and the same slicked-back hair. She thought perhaps this was the model Yoshke meant to emulate. It looked better on Yoshke, truth be told. The gentile was blond with nearly no eyebrows and a mustache too light to really give shape to his face. He looked to Sorel like a nocturnal creature that had crawled from under a fallen log.

She didn't like how he was looking at Adela, either.

"Christian girls have nothing on a real Jewess," he was saying. "Yoshke told me he had business associates who needed to talk to me! But this is a princess! Come, have a seat. Make room for her, you trolls!"

The wave of his hand sent a couple of the gamblers slouching reluctantly to a corner. Adela sat without taking the angry look off her face, and Sorel sat next to her so that if anyone tried to touch either of them, he'd get a knife in the face.

Yoshke, despite there not being enough room on the bench for three, squeezed himself in next to Sorel, while Sam kept standing behind them, quiet as a golem.

"You're Pavlikov?" Adela said. "I'm looking for Isser Jacobs."

Pavlikov blinked and kept blinking for what struck Sorel as an excessive amount of time. She could almost see him arranging a story in his head. "Isser Jacobs? Oh, don't let's talk about that little mosquito. Surely, you're not his sister?"

"I am," said Adela. She took no time to blink and consider, she simply said it. Sorel felt a stir of affection that wasn't entirely hers—a flash of a memory, Adela defending her on a muddy street, the two of them holding hands.

Isser?

He didn't respond, but she could feel him. He was there again. What was keeping him? She could use his help. Surely he'd know what questions to ask Pavlikov to get answers.

"I'm looking for him," said Adela. "He hasn't been home. I heard you know everything that goes on in Esrog."

"Well," said Pavlikov. "Isn't that flattering. I may know a thing or two, but I'm not in the habit of giving away secrets to just anyone—you understand."

Sorel saw where Yoshke got his attitude from. It wasn't any more charming the second time around. "Do you give away secrets to people who beat you at cards?" she asked brashly.

"Alter," said Sam, in a low warning voice.

"Who's this?" said Pavlikov, speaking to Yoshke. "Isser's brother? His rabbi?"

"You couldn't expect a girl to come alone, could you?" said Sorel. "Of course she brought help. Don't be stupid."

"Alter," said Sam again.

"You look like a man who knows how to make bets," said Sorel, looking Pavlikov in the face. "So go on, bet me that I can't beat you at a hand. If I win, tell us all you know about Isser. If you win, we'll just stop bothering you."

"If I win, I'd like a kiss from the Queen of Persia," said Pavlikov.

Sorel was opening her mouth to make a counteroffer when Adela said "Done" and slapped the table. Their audience of sodden gentiles applauded and broke out in delighted laughter.

Sam leaned down to whisper in Sorel's ear. "Are you even any good at cards?"

She had no reason to think so, but Isser, her yetzer-hara, was fully awake now. She could feel him sitting in her skin, looking out through her eyes. She could also feel his indignation. She was being reckless, and he didn't like it.

What kind of mess have you put us in now? he said in her ear. Then, out loud, in her own voice: "I'm very good."

CHAPTER

9

THE GAME WAS DURAK. Sorel had never played it, but watched her own hands take the cards with practiced movements. When Pavlikov looked into her eyes, he frowned, as if he saw something there that gave him pause.

It's like a duel, Isser whispered in her ear.

Do you think a good Jewish girl fights duels? she shot back at him.

I think a good Jewish girl would have thought of that before she issued a challenge, he said. *But you're not a good Jewish girl anyway. So. It's about timing and confidence. You're not very good at timing, but you've got confidence, haven't you?*

He'd been cutting the deck while they talked, throwing aside the low numbered cards. The game needed four, so Yoshke took a hand to their right, and Pavlikov waved Sam to switch places with Adela to their left.

"So you don't think we're cheating you by collaborating," he said, giving Sorel a poisonous grin. "Do you know the game, Moses?"

Sam blinked at him placidly and didn't bother to correct him. "I know the game."

The key is to keep your head. Be patient, Isser was explaining as he dealt them each their hand of six. *You have to have stamina for the endgame. Can you do that?*

Do I have a choice? Sorel asked, watching his hands. They didn't move like hers—she almost didn't recognize them. *Aren't you controlling this?*

It's just that you aren't very cooperative, he said. *You ignored me entirely last night. Don't think I've forgotten. We aren't to focus on Pavlikov. Let him think we can't keep ahold of him. It's Yoshke we're after. Make him miserable.*

Sorel glanced to her right and saw Yoshke looking uncomfortable, frowning at his cards. She didn't think it would be too difficult to make him miserable. Pavlikov had implicitly claimed him for the goyish side of the table, but he was still Jewish, after all, and if she wanted to remind everyone of that she could. And he had the look of a man with a bad starting hand.

I meant in the game, said Isser, in a tone of irony, *but if you want to be rude to him I wouldn't mind that, either.*

Sorel wished she could swat him, but he was inside her head. *Is there a way to stop you from knowing what I'm thinking?*

The pause before he responded made her think there was, but he didn't want her to know about it. *I've never been a dybbuk before, Alter. Maybe ask a rabbi.*

Sorel flipped over the trump with a slap. Hearts. Sam had the first attack with Pavlikov to defend—they weren't playing as teams, despite Pavlikov's sneering suggestion of collaboration. First between Sorel and Pavlikov to discard their hand would be the winner. Sam took forever to choose his card and Isser hissed in Sorel's ear to stop fidgeting. She forced her tapping foot to still.

Let him beat Sam, Isser said, shuffling the cards in their hand into some kind of order. *Then he'll attack Yoshke, and we pile on. It's better playing a hand of four; Pavlikov isn't a good sideways thinker.*

Sure enough, Pavlikov gave them an odd look when they declined to join the attack. So did Yoshke, his eyes lingering on their face as Sam picked up the losing cards. Sorel could feel Isser counting, keeping track of what had been played. It gave her a headache.

"Not much good for a bet if neither of us wins," Pavlikov said. "What's the matter? Bad hand?"

Don't answer that, said Isser. Sorel could feel his focus moving away, and her hands were her own again.

I'm not an idiot, she replied.

Yoshke's got an eight, he said. *But play the seven. Either Sam will play his ten or we can let Yoshke attack us.*

How do you know that? Sorel glanced sideways at Yoshke. *Aren't you in my head?*

Not really. He didn't elaborate. She laid down the card. Yoshke played the eight with a look of relief. Sorel felt Adela at her shoulder, watching, as Sam declined to join the attack.

"What is it you need Isser for, anyway?" said Pavlikov.

"Owes me money," Sorel heard her voice say as she slapped down the cards to ward off Yoshke's attack. "Why? Remembered something after all?"

"If I were him, I'd have skipped town," said Pavlikov, casually.

Adela grabbed Sorel's shoulder for support, leaning forward. "Why?"

Pavlikov shrugged and waved the cards in his hand, as if to remind them that they were playing for the answers. "I don't want to disappoint you, princess, but your brother's got enemies. Not just the authorities, either. If you do find him, I'd tell him to watch his back."

Sorel was trying to remember which cards were in play, but the warmth of Adela's grip on her shoulder was strangely distracting. *Pull yourself together!* Isser hissed.

"Who else?" said Adela. "You?"

"Me?" Pavlikov looked around at his friends, theatrically. "Lads, would I waste my time making an enemy of some petty bookselling Jew?"

There was a murmur of dissent.

"I have bigger fish to fry," said Pavlikov. "What do I care if your people are reading satanic books? The world can go to the devil for all I care."

"But you'd care if you thought someone was muscling in on your turf," said Isser. Their hand couldn't defend; Sorel picked up the cards. "Say, if you thought someone else had counterfeit stamps. You'd care about that, no?"

Pavlikov frowned. "I'd care, but Isser wasn't in that business, and Yoshke here gives me a fair cut—he likes his nose the shape it is, don't you, Yoshke."

"Right," said Yoshke. "Isser wasn't in that business."

"I'd ask your fellow Jews," said Pavlikov, joining the attack on Sam's card. "Remember that bad business when we were all children? That was over books, wasn't it?"

"What bad business?" said Sorel, before Isser could respond—she felt his irritation. "Between the Hasidim and the merchants?"

"All I remember is when they fished the man out of the river," said Pavlikov. "All us kids went down to watch them do it, didn't we, Yoshke."

Sam said something under his breath, Sorel thought she heard Hebrew. Probably a blessing for the long-dead man.

"I didn't actually see him," said Yoshke, glancing up at Adela as if to ward off disapproval.

"No one ever proved it was Jews that did that," said Sam.

"Did what, for God's sake?" said Sorel. "I don't remember this at all."

"Not from Esrog, are you," said Pavlikov, as if Esrog were the center of the world.

"As it happens, I'm not. Not that it's any business of yours."

"There was a miracle worker here before the rebbe they have now," explained Sam, gently. Sorel was almost as irritated by the helpful tone as she had been by everyone talking around her. "They found him in the river drowned, may he rest in peace."

"Everyone knows it was the Jews that did it," said Pavlikov. He was grinning, and the grin made Sorel play a trump from her hand to take the grin away. She felt Isser's irritation at her impulsiveness.

He's trying to make you angry, Alter. Ignore it. Wait.

"Why would the Jews have done it?" she demanded, ignoring him instead.

"God knows," said Pavlikov.

"It can't have anything to do with Isser anyway," said Adela, though her voice was tense. "That was between the Hasidim and the kahal. Isser doesn't have anything to do with either."

"He has something to do with one hasid," said Yoshke, doubtfully. He was holding his cards loosely, almost as if he'd forgotten he was playing. He looked a bit sick.

"It was that rich bastard from the estate over to the south," said Pavlikov, speaking over Yoshke. "That's who everyone said was behind it. What's his name, the lumber merchant."

"Kalman," said Yoshke.

CHAPTER
10

Sorel tried to speak at the same time as Isser, and they choked on the words, coughing until Adela slapped them on the back.

"It can't be Kalman!" Sorel exclaimed. "Why would he do that?"

Pavlikov shrugged.

"Because he's in charge of the kahal," said Yoshke. "So he says what goes and what doesn't, at least for the Jews. That's why. It was a squabble between the Hasidim and the merchants, that's what everyone says. About who'd get to lead the Esroger Jews."

"Yes, all right." Sorel slapped down a card without really thinking, annoyed at everyone, though she couldn't have said why. It wasn't as if she liked her father. But to think of him ordering a murder? It was impossible. "So he's a leader. But he wouldn't have had someone killed!"

"You know him?" Sam asked.

Sorel sputtered for a second.

God preserve us, said Isser, exasperated and unhelpful. *No one likes Kalman, stop defending him.*

"I don't know him," she said. "Only he, well, he gives tzedakah for the widows and orphans in my village."

"Guilty conscience," said Pavlikov, knowingly.

"Ridiculous," said Sorel. "He's friends with the rebbe, too, isn't he? His daughter's married the rebbe's son."

"That's politics," said Yoshke. "Everyone knows it. Even the Christians." With a nod toward Pavlikov.

Sorel bit her tongue to stop from saying that Christians having heard a rumor did not make that rumor true.

"None of this has anything to do with Isser," said Sam, his calm tone cutting through the argument. "And it's old news, anyway, from when the lot of you were in short pants."

"Maybe Kalman doesn't like modern politics," said Pavlikov. "German politics. That's most of what Isser sells, isn't it? Revolution. Not that I've read it."

"Isser sells whatever people want to buy, like anyone," said Yoshke. Sorel felt an odd spark of affection for him—not hers. Isser's, touched at the unexpected defense. "And Christians want to read the German pamphlets too."

"So what you're saying is that the whole of Esrog could know where Isser is, because the whole of Esrog either bought from him or didn't want people buying from him," said Adela. "But no one actually knows. Is that it?"

"That's a question to be answered when your yeshiva boy picks up his next hand," said Pavlikov, winking at her. Sorel seethed. Her hand was indeed swollen, certainly more than Sam's next to her; she wished they were playing as teams after all, as Sam or Yoshke going out would have no effect on the bet.

So much for being good at cards, she thought at Isser.

You're the one who made a couple of bad plays in a row. His voice was sharp. *Calm down and let me lead again.*

I'm not stopping you!

You are stopping me. I was trying to speak. She could feel him wrestling her for control, now that she stopped to think about it. Tugging at her from inside her bones. She huffed out an irritable breath and tried to recapture the feeling of freedom she'd got the first time Isser took over, when he leapt from the window on her feet.

Thank you, he said, in a singularly ungrateful tone, and her hands started to reshuffle their cards without her. She could feel Adela's tension where the other girl stood close behind them. Isser was counting cards again, and Sorel's attention wandered. Yoshke, to their right, looked uncomfortable still. Sam looked as if he were thinking very hard as he frowned at his cards. Pavlikov's gang of card players had gotten bored and wandered back to their own tables, though one or two of them seemed to be listening, more alert and less drunk than the others.

"I think you're lying," Isser said to Pavlikov. "I think someone told you Isser was selling counterfeit stamps and you got angry and killed him."

Pavlikov laughed, a loud, shocked exclamation. Adela drew in a breath.

"Killed him? I didn't need to kill him! If I had that kind of trouble from him, I'd just run him off. You think he's that important?"

"He was blackmailing you," Isser said. Sorel tried to read him, but she couldn't tell if he meant it or if he was just trying to provoke Pavlikov into a confession.

"With what?" said Pavlikov. "Don't be absurd. Even if he had one of my secrets, who would he tell?"

"The kahal," said Isser. "The same Kalman you hate so much. The rebbe, even. And they'd tell the governor."

"Tell the governor what?" said Pavlikov. "The governor doesn't care what any of us do."

"That you've been smuggling arms from Poland," said Isser.

The room went silent. Suddenly everyone, even the drunkest of Pavlikov's friends, was listening. Yoshke moved away from Sorel-Isser, as if they were suddenly poisonous.

"I'm out," said Sam, into the silence. He slid his final card onto the table and held up his empty hands.

"Get out," Pavlikov snapped, raising his voice. No one moved. "Get out! Everyone out!" He waved his hands, shooing the drunken audience away. "Mind your own business! You too," he snapped at Yoshke, who hadn't moved. And to Sam, "And you."

The room cleared. Adela stood firm at Sorel's back.

Pavlikov laid down his cards and leaned forward on his elbows, staring into Sorel's face.

"Who have you been talking to?"

Isser shrugged their shoulders. "I thought we were playing for answers."

"Damn the game!" Pavlikov snapped. "The bet is off. Was it you?" He looked up at Adela. "Did he tell you? You're keeping his secrets?"

"Are you planning to kill me if I am?" said Adela.

The room felt suddenly much larger and colder than it had been before. Sorel wished she could reach for the knife, but Isser still had control of her hands—of her whole body. It felt less like freedom now, but she didn't know how she'd wrestled control back from him before, and he ignored her desperate internal warning.

"I don't touch women," said Pavlikov. "But I'm devilish tempted to do it."

"She didn't know anything until just now," said Isser. "Leave her out of it. He told me. What, you thought he wouldn't have any safeguards? In case he disappeared?" He put his own cards down and leaned forward, matching Pavlikov's posture. This close Sorel could see her own face, strangely unfamiliar, reflected in the young man's eyes. "Where'd you put the body, Jurek?"

She expected another denial, but Pavlikov was searching her face, his expression shifting to something she hadn't seen before. Doubt.

He'd seen something in her eyes that unsettled him.

"There's no body," he said, sitting up, putting distance between them. "There's no body, you damned madman. I don't know where he is."

"Alter—" Adela started to say.

With sudden speed, Isser leapt to his feet and threw aside the table with a strength Sorel hadn't known she had. It was a solid thing, not a flimsy card table, and it hit the wall with a crash. Adela screamed and Pavlikov scrambled backward as Isser reached for him, catching him by the collar.

"Where is the body?" he shouted again. "What did you do with my body?"

"It wasn't me!" Pavlikov yelled, all his confidence gone. "Virgin Mary protect me, I don't know where it is!"

Isser backed him up to the wall, pressing him to the tobacco-stained paneling. "But you knew I was dead. Didn't you. Didn't you!"

Pavlikov was babbling now, incoherent. Sorel scrambled for a hold over Isser, but it was like trying to catch a shadow. She couldn't even feel her own limbs.

"Alter!" Adela screamed.

Someone was pounding at the door, rattling the lock. Sorel did not think it had been locked, before.

"If you didn't do it, then who did?" Isser hissed in Pavlikov's face, ice cold. "Who am I looking for?"

"I don't know," said Pavlikov. "I don't know, I don't know— ask Yoshke."

"We asked Yoshke already, and he said to ask you. Why else would I be here?"

The locked door rattled again, and then there was a loud bang and the shouting voices outside stopped. Adela had ducked, catching at Sorel's shoulder.

"Someone's shot the door!" she yelled in their ear, in Yiddish. "Stop it, Isser, we have to leave!"

The sound of her voice knocked something loose, and suddenly, Sorel had control again. She tore herself away from Pavlikov, grabbed Adela by the elbow, and ran for the window. She didn't want to contend with Pavlikov's friends in the hallway, much less with a gun. They leapt out the window and hit the tin roof of a shed in the alley, Adela wrapping her arms around Sorel as they rolled down the slanted roof. They landed hard in cold muck, Adela on top of her knocking the air from Sorel's lungs.

"What is wrong with you!" Adela exclaimed, breathless, rolling off and getting to her feet. She offered a hand and Sorel took it, struggling upright and gasping for a breath. She felt bruised, though not as bruised as she thought she should—some of the mad, wild strength still lingered from Isser's take-over. Adela dragged her down the alley and away, making turns at random, both of them stumbling in the dark.

CHAPTER

11

SOREL AND ADELA WERE still holding hands when at last, breathless, they came to a stop on the edge of a better-lit street. The noise of shouting and the barking of dogs had faded behind them, and Sorel had caught no more gunshots. She leaned against a wall to catch her breath.

Adela let go of Sorel's hand and Sorel had only a second to miss her touch before Adela laid her hands over Sorel's cheeks instead.

"It is you, isn't it?" she said. "Isser. It's you, somehow. You're dead?"

"Sorry," said Sorel. She couldn't find Isser anywhere—it was like that burst of anger had burnt him out. "Yes. He isn't here right now, he's—I don't know, he comes and goes."

Adela searched her face for a long time, looking for traces of Isser perhaps. Her hands were pleasantly cool on Sorel's face, her eyes dark pools of shadow. "Then who are you?"

"Nobody," said Sorel. She wasn't sure why she didn't confess her secret. She liked Adela, she wanted to be honest, but somehow it didn't feel any less dishonest to say she was Kalman's runaway daughter. "I mean, Alter. Let's stick with Alter. Isser just, I don't know. Found me. And now I'm helping him."

Adela stepped away and brushed her sweaty hair off her forehead. "We shouldn't have left Sam. In a room with all those goyim."

"And Yoshke?" Sorel asked.

"Yoshke can go to hell. I half think he wanted to set us up, anyway. But he'll be fine. He always is." She made a choked sound, like a laugh gone wrong. "Although, I used to think that about Isser."

"You've known each other a long time," said Sorel. Her chest ached, and not only with the running. She'd never had a friend, not really, and certainly not a friend like what Adela and Isser seemed to be to each other.

"Forever," said Adela.

They stayed there in silence for a minute or two, until their hearts stopped pounding. Sorel started to notice all the places she ached again—her ribs now joining her legs and feet, and a twinge in her right wrist that she thought she must have landed on in the fall. She brushed mud from her trousers absentmindedly. She'd never stopped to think why the people she saw in the street—peasants, children, poorer Jews—were always muddy. But here she was, practically fresh from the bathhouse, and filthy already.

Filthy and hungry, again. Her stomach gnawed at her as if she hadn't eaten in days. Where did one get food on the night after shabbes? She could suddenly think of nothing else.

"Should we wait for Sam somewhere?" Adela asked. "Where would he go to look for us?"

"I don't know." Sorel checked that her satchel still hung from her shoulder and dug through it, hoping for crumbs, but she'd eaten them all already. "I don't know Esrog. Where can we go?"

Adela gave it some thought. "Isser's apartment. I should look at it, see if there's anything. If he meant it about the counterfeit stamps. That was him talking?"

"Yes," said Sorel. "But it's torn apart in there, I don't think you'd find anything." Then her hand caught something cool and sharp in her pocket, and she straightened up. "It can't have been Jews that did it!"

"Why not?"

Sorel took the mezuzah case from her pocket and showed it to her. It must have slipped out of the pouch Sam put it in, and the edge had bitten her fingers. "This! They tore it off his door. Father—Kalman would never do that. An observant Jew would never."

Adela touched it gently, her eyes sad. "Not an observant Jew, I suppose. There's a few who might, though. If they're angry enough that they're Jewish."

"You should take it," said Sorel.

"I don't think it even belonged to Isser, really. It would have been his landlord who put it up."

"Take it anyway. Sam said it would protect me, or something. I don't feel protected. It isn't keeping the dybbuk out of my head."

"I think maybe we shouldn't tell Sam about Isser," said Adela, taking the mezuzah and tucking it into her pocket. "If we find him again. He'll think we're both mad."

"Of course not," said Sorel. She hadn't been planning to tell Sam. He looked at her too closely, and she worried if she told him anything more than she had to, he would see right through her.

"I still think we should go now," said Adela. "There might be something I'd see that anyone else would have missed."

"Right. Of course."

"And it's a dry place to sleep," she added, looking suddenly exhausted. "Come on. I think I know the way."

IT WAS WELL PAST DARK and they were both dragging their feet when they got to Isser's street. It occurred to Sorel that there would be no light and nothing to eat—her insides continued to gnaw at her viciously—and so she sent Adela up ahead of her and went to knock at the lamp-lit window of one of the neighbors. There she was able to trade a couple of coins for a taper and a loaf of bread with some boiled eggs, although the husband who'd answered her knock kept looking at her oddly as he collected the food. She apologized for the interruption and wished him a good week before he could ask her any questions.

She found Adela sweeping broken pieces of crockery out the door of Isser's apartment, onto the balcony.

"I brought a candle to light the fire," she said, through a mouthful of boiled egg. She'd thought she might faint if she waited to eat it.

"Good," said Adela. "Wait out here a minute, would you? I'm soaked; I need to get out of these skirts."

"Oh. All right."

Adela shut the door in her face and Sorel stood on the spot, feeling very silly, picking chunks off the bread. Was she supposed to guard the doorway? Adela was awfully bold. Sorel didn't think she would have told a boy she was changing, not when she'd been a girl—not that she'd had much opportunity. Why was she so flustered? It wasn't a complicated request. She was just standing. The door was shut; she couldn't even hear Adela moving around inside. It occurred to her that she oughtn't try to hear her, and she turned and went to sit at the top of the steps. She focused very hard on peeling another egg while she waited for the door to open again.

When it did, Adela was dressed in what must have been Isser's clothes: a man's shirt and vest, and a pair of trousers that fit tight at her hips, rolled up at the ankles to show her wool stockings. She was holding her dress in her arms and gave it a fearsome shake over the edge of the balcony. She didn't look at Sorel, which was just as well, because it took Sorel a second to realize she was staring.

"I was freezing," said Adela, by way of explanation. "I've started a fire. Have you eaten everything?"

Sorel held out the peeled egg to her, sheepish. "It's just boiled eggs and challah."

They ate the rest of it sitting on the floor by the little stove in Isser's room. Neither was awake enough to talk much, and Sorel thought she'd start weeping if anything stopped her from sleeping.

"I'll look around in the morning," Adela said, when they'd eaten the last crumbs and warmed themselves a little. "It's too dark now. Isser . . . he's not here, is he?"

Sorel shook her head.

"You look a bit different, I think, when he's here." She tilted her head, frowning at Sorel's face. Sorel felt her cheeks warm and was glad it wouldn't be visible in the firelight. "Something in your eyes."

"I don't know why he's not there all the time, but it feels like he isn't."

Adela nodded. There was another silence. Sorel tried to think when she might have contracted a dybbuk. Was it the night of her wedding, when he'd made her jump out the window? But he'd already felt so much like part of herself.

She'd fought with her father constantly since the engagement, coming up with reason after reason why it wouldn't work—she was too young, the rebbe's son was too young, her mother wouldn't have approved, the rebbe's son was too learned and she too secular, everything she could think of. Kalman had an answer for all of it. Yes they were young, but they needn't live together all of the time after the wedding, not until the rebbe's son finished his studies. And yes, Kalman would be responsible for supporting them during that time, but he was responsible for Sorel already. And it was prestigious to support a scholar—a mitzvah and an honor—especially when the scholar would surely grow up to perform miracles, not that Kalman really believed in miracles, but God forbid he admit it. As for her mother's approval, he had never wanted or needed it. He and Sorel were stuck with one another as father and daughter, absent a son to carry on the business or a better daughter who would not make the smallest thing a tzureh for him.

Sorel had argued that her wedding, her life, was no small thing, and indeed it had been a tzureh for her first so her father shouldn't complain about her turning the tzureh around on him. Then she'd slammed the door and gone out riding and fallen off her horse in the woods, and while she was lying there in the underbrush it had occurred to her that if she had to marry the rebbe's son, she would die.

Was it then that Isser had come to her? Had he been dead already?

"What makes a dybbuk take someone?" she asked, staring at the glow from inside the stove rather than looking at Adela's face. "I never really learned all that—mothers' stuff, bobe-mayses."

"I don't know," said Adela. "A letter missing from a mezuzah?"

She glanced over at the windowsill when she said it, and Sorel saw that Adela had placed Isser's mezuzah case there.

"That's what keeps demons out, God forbid," Adela said. "Or anyway that's what I always heard. If you have a good kosher mezuzah, and you, as a man, if you wear your fringes properly."

Sorel glanced down at her hips. She'd forgotten she was wearing tzitzis. She wasn't sure how the knots were meant to look, so she couldn't tell if they were properly done or not. But that wouldn't have mattered when she was a girl, anyway.

She couldn't ask if Adela had insights for how a dybbuk came on a woman. That would be a strange and revealing question. "I just always thought it was madness. You know, a sickness of the head—not really a dybbuk at all."

Adela shrugged. "In that room, when you attacked Pavlikov . . . well, all right, it looked a bit like madness, but it was freezing cold in there, and the door was locked when no one had locked it. Remember how cramped and stuffy it was when we came in? It was cold as midwinter all of a sudden. And then you broke through the window like a golem."

"Maybe the door just locked on its own," said Sorel, aware she was arguing just for the sake of arguing, that she could think of nothing to make Isser's presence less real. "A latch that was stuck, something like that. And drafts, once everyone went out of the room."

"I don't think so," said Adela.

"No," Sorel admitted, with a sigh. "I don't think so either."

"There's two blankets," said Adela. "Let's rest, while we can. We will try again in the morning."

CHAPTER

12

SOREL WOKE ON THE FLOOR by the stove, feeling like she'd been trampled by horses in her sleep. Adela must have woken and already gone out, because she'd left her blanket neatly folded on the bed. Sorel tossed hers next to it and pulled her boots back over her protesting feet.

She was drinking from the well in the courtyard and dreaming of a hearty breakfast when Adela came back, dressed in her skirts again with Isser's shirt on top and a basket under her arm. Her cheeks were pink, as if she'd been running.

"Oh, good, you're awake," she said. "We have to go over to the Great Synagogue, something's happening."

"What's happening?" Sorel asked, standing up straight, her hand going to her pocket to check for the knife automatically.

"The women I talked to weren't sure, but there's been some excitement overnight. Something to do with searching the river." She took a slab of kugel from the basket, wrapped in a towel, and handed it to Sorel as she spoke. "They said someone from the next street over is in the women's chevra kadisha. They woke the neighbors in the middle of the night with their commotion."

"Women's chevra kadisha?" said Sorel through a mouthful of kugel. "So it isn't Isser."

"So?" said Adela. "Don't you want to know what's happening?"

She did, but it hadn't seemed quite appropriate to be interested. Adela's lack of hesitation encouraged her. "Do they find a lot of people in the river in Esrog? My father never mentioned it happening."

"Your father would know?" Adela asked. "I certainly don't. It doesn't seem likely that it happens every Shabbat."

Sorel swallowed the last of the kugel as they started walking. They weren't the only ones headed toward the Great Synagogue—it seemed whatever gossip Adela had picked up was spreading fast. The atmosphere felt similar to the other day when Sorel had joined the crowd headed to her own wedding feast. Only this time, there was a certain tension in the air that hadn't been there before. Rather than talking aloud and laughing, like the old women on the way to the feast, this was a crowd of whispers.

The courtyard of the synagogue itself was packed with people, all straining their ears toward the steps as if they expected someone to come out and make an announcement. An enterprising middle-aged woman had set herself up to sell candied almonds and raisins out of a basket on the side and was doing roaring business for an audience of little girls and cheder boys. Sorel dug in her pocket for a coin and went to join them, Adela at her elbow.

"What's going on?" Sorel asked. "I heard someone was dead in the river."

"Kalman the lumber merchant's daughter, God forbid!" said the woman, quite cheerfully. "Someone's put the evil eye on our tzadik, I shouldn't wonder!"

"It can't be," said Sorel. She handed over her coin and received a sticky paper packet.

"It is," the woman insisted. "Everyone's saying so. They found her wedding dress. Everyone saw it, because they brought it to show the rebbe's attendants last night, and my Perla said she saw a hasid riding for Kalman's estate after havdalah, and now we're all waiting for Kalman and the rebbe, God bless them, to arrive and look at the body."

"Why are we all here, then?" Sorel asked, through a mouthful of sugary almonds. "There's a corpse in the synagogue?"

"Not in the synagogue," said the woman, as if she were speaking to a rather dim child. "They've got her in the mortuary at the poorhouse behind, poor child, may we be spared such sorrows. But there's no room in that alleyway, and anyway if there's ever news to be heard you can hear it on Synagogue Street, everyone knows it. You're new to Esrog?"

"Yes," said Sorel. "I came for the wedding feast. To get the rebbe's blessing, you know, because I'm a poor orphan."

Adela gave her a look that made her think her tone hadn't been quite right for what she was saying. Maybe it was because she was eating candy while she said it. She tried to surreptitiously lick the last of the sugar off her hand as she tucked the rest of the packet away for later.

"Well, God forbid it is Kalman's daughter, that is, the rebbe's daughter-in-law," said the woman. She was still handing out candy to small, grubby-faced customers as she talked, and her God forbid didn't sound any more sincere than Sorel's poor orphan. "It's a great blessing to the community to have that wedding."

"Right," said Sorel. "Because it means the Hasidim and the kahal aren't rivals anymore. Isn't that it?"

"That's right. And because if they're family, no one can spread those nasty rumors about Kalman Senderovich anymore! Not that any of us ever believed them." She gave Sorel a sidelong, hopeful look.

Sorel resigned herself to yet another Esroger telling her stories about her father. "What nasty rumors?"

"That he had the rebbe's father murdered years ago! Oh, it was a terrible time. A time of devils! There was a goat born in Kuritsev with three eyes that spring—my own mother saw it. I was just a young bride then."

"I'm from Kuritsev," said Adela. "I never heard of a three-eyed goat. Alter, come on, I want to get closer."

She dragged Sorel away by the back of her coat, employing some impressive elbow jabs to clear them a path through the crowd toward the front of the synagogue. Sorel ducked her head and pulled her cap lower when she recognized the same lieutenant of the rebbe that she'd spoken to on her wedding day, the one who'd been annoyed to hear she'd gone missing.

Adela dragged her past a knot of skinny teenage Hasidim and wedged the two of them into a corner by the door to the women's section. Even this close, the whispered consultation of the men in the doorway was impossible to catch—too many people were speaking on all sides. Sorel leaned forward and strained her ears and caught her own name.

"It is Kalman's daughter," she reported to Adela. "But that can't be right!"

"Why not?" Adela asked. She was frowning into the crowd as if she'd just caught sight of something.

Sorel opened her mouth to explain that it was impossible for Kalman's daughter to have drowned in the river—then stopped. She had no reasonable explanation for thinking so, unless she wanted to explain that she knew exactly where the body of Kalman's daughter was located. And for some reason, she really did not want to give up that secret.

"I just . . . I don't think it's her," she said, hearing the lack of confidence in her own voice. "I mean first of all, how could it have happened?"

"Isser, look," said Adela. "That's him, isn't it?"

"What?" Sorel blinked, looking around. Adela was pointing, although subtly, with her hand held up to her chest as if she didn't want to alert the person she'd seen. Sorel followed her gaze to the group of boys in hasidic gabardines. They all seemed to be gathered around one in particular, which Sorel hadn't noticed before. One of his friends was patting him consolingly on the shoulder.

"What's he doing here?" Sorel exclaimed, before she could stop herself.

She was standing barely twenty feet from her fiancé.

"It's him, isn't it?" said Adela.

"Him who?" said Sorel, catching herself. "Isser isn't here right now. I haven't heard from him."

Not even in her dreams, she realized now. Had he broken himself? Surely scaring Pavlikov hadn't been all he wanted. He'd needed to find his body.

"The one whose father paid for Isser to take his place at school," said Adela. At the same time that Sorel, looking again, realized something else and said,

"The hasid who looks like a weasel!"

He really did look a bit like a weasel, poor thing, once you considered that weasels' dark shining eyes were quite sweet. He was a bit younger than Sorel, but he'd always seemed even younger than he was—not that they'd ever talked that much. Mainly because he seemed unable to speak to or look at her. She'd never gotten this good a look at his face, in fact, because he kept his eyes glued to his own toes whenever they were in a room together.

"His name's Shulem-Yontif, poor bastard," she said, and cursed herself again for speaking without thinking. "Uh, I think. Isser maybe mentioned it."

"That's right," said Adela, not noticing the stumble. "Shulem-Yontif. He looks a bit . . ."

She trailed off.

"A bit of a shlimazl?" Sorel suggested. "Well, everyone's saying his wife's dead, aren't they."

Shulem-Yontif, indeed looked like he'd been crying, although Sorel couldn't imagine why. It wasn't as if he'd ever really had a conversation with her. And he couldn't have been looking forward to performing the mitzvah of man and wife with her, surely. She'd been as unpleasant to him as she possibly could in their every interaction.

She almost felt bad about it now. With neither of their fathers standing by, he looked very young and innocent, and easy to knock over.

"He's the rebbe's son?" Adela asked. "I didn't know that. We should talk to him."

Sorel almost screamed that they definitely shouldn't, but it was too late. Adela didn't wait for anyone's approval—or, for that matter, to consider whether a group of yeshiva boys in black coats would even speak to her in public. Sorel was forced to run after her.

"Adela, you can't talk to him in public. I'll get him." She couldn't be sure Shulem-Yontif wouldn't recognize her, but she was sure she couldn't convince Adela it wasn't worth talking to him. "If you go in the alley and wait, I'll bring him. He won't talk to you with people watching."

Adela huffed but stopped and turned toward the alley Sorel had pointed to. "Fine. Just don't let him go without talking."

This left Sorel alone with the problem of how to convince Shulem-Yontif to follow her into an alleyway instead of sticking around to hear whatever announcement the crowd was hoping for. She dithered for a moment and then decided that since she was a boy, she could be direct. No need for cleverness, just bully him. He looked like he'd easily submit to bullying.

She marched up to him and grabbed him by the arm. "Shulem-Yontif! I need to talk to you!"

The boys all goggled at her, wide-eyed.

"What?" said Shulem-Yontif. "Who? What?"

Sorel didn't bother to explain. She just yanked him by the elbow until he gave in and followed her, leaving the rest of the group to stare after them. They pushed through the crowd easily enough but at the mouth of the narrow alley—nearly blocked by a rain barrel they'd have to squeeze past—Shulem-Yontif suddenly dug in his heels.

"Did Yoshke send you?" he squeaked. "I already talked to Yoshke! I don't have anything more to say to him!"

"Yoshke did not send me," said Sorel, adjusting her grip so she could push him ahead of her like a recalcitrant goat. They wrestled for a moment and then he gave up again, or rather he switched to a strategy of going limp in her arms, so that she had to drag him into the alley where Adela was waiting, half-hidden among strings of laundry that criss-crossed the small space.

Shulem-Yontif seemed to have expected a gang of armed men or fighting dogs. He breathed a sigh of relief at the sight of just one girl, but then an expression of confusion crossed his face.

"Guess what," said Sorel, positioning herself at his back so he couldn't slip away, and so he wouldn't be looking at her face as Adela talked. "Yoshke lied to us. He's talked to Shulem-Yontif already."

"What did Yoshke talk to you about?" Adela asked.

"I told him everything!" said Shulem-Yontif, desperately. "I haven't seen Isser! And he didn't give the book back, he has it—and I don't even know what he wanted it for, so don't ask me!"

"Slow down," said Adela. "I'm Adela, by the way. You're Shulem-Yontif?"

"I don't want to talk to you," said Shulem-Yontif, who was looking anywhere but Adela's face, even craning his neck around to try to look at Sorel. Sorel was rather enjoying the role of enforcer, folding her arms and glaring at him.

"We're not going to hurt you," said Adela. "I'm just a friend of Isser's and I'm looking for him. I'm not a friend of Yoshke's, either. Yoshke said he didn't know who Isser's Hasidic friend was, but that was a lie, wasn't it? He knew it was you."

"It's a sin to speak to a woman in seclusion," Shulem-Yontif mumbled.

"We aren't in seclusion," said Adela. "We're in public, and Alter is here."

Shulem-Yontif looked around at Sorel again. He did not seem reassured by her as a chaperone. Sorel felt an odd spark of a memory—sitting with Shulem-Yontif over a book, the two of them having a real conversation. It was accompanied by the same warmth of affection she'd briefly felt for Yoshke, through Isser.

So, he and Isser had been friends. The boy had strange taste.

"What's this about a book?" she asked. "Yoshke asked you about a book?"

Shulem-Yontif wrung his hands, looking between them for a moment before heaving a sigh of resignation. "Yes, there was—he asked for a book from my father's library. My father, do you know him?"

"Everyone knows your father's the Esroger tzadik," said Sorel, ignoring the fact that Adela clearly hadn't known it a few minutes ago. "What book?"

"A book," said Shulem-Yontif again, uselessly. "A, well, God forbid, a very illegal book. But a holy book! A holy book. Well, I'm not allowed to read it. You can't read it unless you're married, so I didn't. But Isser needed it. He said he was just borrowing it! But he stole it! You should tell him I'm not his friend anymore."

"We will if we find him," said Sorel. Isser's affection and her own grudging pity were knotted together in her chest and making her, strangely, want to throw Shulem-Yontif in a puddle. "When was this? And Yoshke asked for it, too? So Yoshke knew."

Shulem-Yontif nodded.

"How did this happen?" Adela asked. "How did Isser even know your father had an illegal book?"

"Well, he knows he has a lot of illegal books," said Shulem-Yontif. "He buys them—my father buys them from him. Often. So of course he knew. But Isser asked for this one, specifically, and he promised me he'd give it back before my father ever knew, only he didn't, and I told him it had to be before my wedding because I'm supposed to go to the woods with my wife, I mean, to live with Kalman the lumber merchant, so I wouldn't be there to put the book back. But the wedding didn't even happen and now my wife is dead!"

This last sentence was on a rising pitch and volume, ending abruptly in a sob. He hid his face in his hands, wailing.

Adela looked like she wanted to reach out and comfort him but stopped herself. She gave Sorel a sharp look that Sorel did not understand.

"Maybe it isn't your wife," said Sorel, stiffly. "I mean, who's even taken a good look at the body?"

This didn't seem to help. Shulem-Yontif started chanting something in Hebrew—she thought it was a psalm.

"Why were you and Isser talking to each other to begin with?" she asked, trying to change the subject. "He's not a hasid. Just because he sold books?"

"He's been teaching me to read in Russian," said Shulem-Yontif, in a small voice. "Don't tell my father."

"Really?" said Sorel, intrigued despite herself. This was a depth she had not expected from the rebbe's obedient son.

"We read poetry," said Shulem-Yontif, as if admitting to the greatest of sins. He was blushing furiously. Sorel wished Isser would wake up so she could talk to him—she suddenly had a lot of questions.

Shulem-Yontif went on, "I asked him to teach me. He was always coming by! And he's so—well, he's different. Can you please tell him to bring that book back?"

"Of course we will," said Adela gently. "But can you think of anything else? Did Yoshke say anything about where Isser has been?"

Shulem-Yontif shook his head. "Just that he hasn't been around and people are looking for him and Yoshke wanted the book. Which he shouldn't even know about, by the way!" He lifted his head with a sudden spark of indignation. "It was meant to be a secret!"

"Isser's bad at keeping promises," said Adela. "I'm sorry he did that to you."

Shulem-Yontif didn't answer, but he looked as if he would have liked to thank her.

"You can go now," said Sorel, stepping aside as much as she could in the narrow space. "If that's really all you know."

"Wait, no it isn't," said Adela. "What's the book called, and what does it look like?"

"It's called Sefer Dumah," said Shulem-Yontif. "The Book of the Angel of Silence. And it's just a book." He held up his hands to indicate a smallish size. "Bound in red leather. There's nothing on the cover and it's tied shut with a ribbon. And it's very old," he added, wrinkling his nose. "It smells."

"Thank you," said Adela. "Now you can go. And we won't share your secret if you don't tell anyone you saw us, all right?"

"Promise," said Shulem-Yontif, and squirmed past Sorel and the rain barrel to disappear into the crowd again.

"So?" said Sorel. Adela looked like she was thinking, her arms folded and eyebrows knit as she gazed at the mud where Shulem-Yontif had been standing.

"So," said Adela, "now we know Isser had two secrets."

CHAPTER

13

FROM THE WAY Shulem-Yontif talked about it, Isser had thought the book would be immediately recognizable as important, a weighty tome bound in leather, perhaps with embossed lettering. But it was nothing like that. It was barely thicker than the chapbooks he sold every day, block printed on cheap rag with fraying edges and charcoal-dust fingerprints on the cover. The one thing that stood out was that it reeked of camphor, making him gag when he inhaled too close to the pages.

"This is it?" he asked, weighing it in his hand again.

"That's it," said Shulem-Yontif.

"It's so ordinary." He didn't know why he was disappointed. This would be much easier to carry, much easier to hide. He flipped it open and checked the binding. Three simple stitches. He already knew how he'd disguise it.

"Well," said Shulem-Yontif, in a tone that told Isser he'd been planning out a narrative in his head. Shulem-Yontif, poor thing, had hardly any adventures in his life, but he was always dreaming of ways to make things sound adventurous. He must have been so thrilled when Isser handed him the real thing—an actual adventure with theft, intrigue, betrayal. Like something from a novel. "You see, my father showed it to me once in particular, so that I'd know that I'm never, ever to touch this book or read it, and certainly not learn anything from it."

"He didn't think telling you about the secret book would make you want to read it?" Isser asked. "I mean, couldn't he just not tell you he had a forbidden book to begin with?"

Shulem-Yontif blinked, thrown off his rhythm by the interruption. "Why would he think that? I never disobey him."

Isser shook his head. "God bless you, Shulem-Yontif."

"Well, anyway, he keeps it in a box in his study, locked up. And he very rarely opens it. Only on holidays! I think. Not that I'm always there when he's in his study, but I've seen him take it out on holidays. Always on Shavuot—so you have to bring it back by then. Promise?"

"Right," said Isser. He was quite sure that by Shavuot the book would no longer be in his hands, one way or another, and he doubted he'd be here to face Shulem-Yontif's disappointment.

"So what I had to do was get the key to the box, and sneak into his study, and open it, and do you know what I did then? I replaced it!" Shulem-Yontif beamed at him, delighted by this bit of improvisation, and Isser smiled weakly back. "I replaced it with one of your pamphlets. A story by Ayzik Meyer Dik."

Isser opened his mouth to protest—one of my pamphlets?—but bit his tongue. Shulem-Yontif, poor thing, was doing his best.

Still, if the rebbe opened the box and found a bit of Yiddish social criticism in place of his sacred angel book . . . he would know. He'd know it was Isser, and he'd think Isser was laughing at him.

He couldn't blame Shulem-Yontif for it. The boy had no head for disobedience, he wouldn't understand.

"Thanks, Shuli," Isser said, and tucked the Sefer Dumah into his vest. "You're a mensch."

BACK IN HIS ROOM over the stables, Isser stacked his kettle and saucepan in front of the door so that anyone trying to get in would cause a racket, covered the window with his coat, and set the lamp on the table.

The pungent camphor scent from the Sefer seemed to fill the whole cramped space when he laid it out in the light. It surprised him that it was printed at all—there must be other copies somewhere, or at least there must once have been copies, despite Shulem-Yontif's insistence that it was the only one in the world. He didn't recognize the letterforms, though. He thought someone might have stamped each page as a whole, from a single block, though he couldn't think why they'd go through the trouble. He recognized on a few of the pages the smudged marks at the corners that you'd get from an improperly carved woodblock.

There was an illustration too, in the middle, but he couldn't make any sense of it; it was just a tangle of shadows, lines that suggested a sense of movement as of wings or horses' legs, something swift, but nothing definable. Was it the shape of the angel the text was meant to bind? He vaguely recalled that angels were supposed to be invisible, or you weren't meant to look at them, like the kohanim giving a blessing in shul. He'd looked at them a few times, having no father to stop him and no holy fear to compensate. They were just barefoot old men to him. *Angels*, he thought, *might be equally disappointing.*

The text itself, the meaning of it, was obscure. He wished Shulem-Yontif would have at least glanced at it, with a yeshiva boy's eye, to give Isser a broad idea of what he was looking at. It was almost like poetry, interrupted by strings of Hebrew letters whose vowels he couldn't begin to guess at.

There was no clear explanation of what the book did. He wanted to understand what he was doing before he continued. He didn't like the idea of being led into something unaware, simply trusting that it was the right thing to do. His grudge against the rebbe did not necessarily translate to believing that Kalman Senderovich knew better how to protect the community. The thought that Kalman believed this book meant anything at all was unusual. Kalman wasn't a superstitious man. There had to be something more to it, something Isser wasn't seeing.

Shulem-Yontif was the only religious Jew he'd trust with a secret. He couldn't ask him. He'd already asked him too much, and Shulem-Yontif's improvised substitution might give Isser away sooner than he'd planned, so he felt even less confident in asking the boy for help.

He sat for a while staring at the pages, biting his nails. Then he got up and took his sewing kit from the cabinet on the wall, moved the chair over, and tugged the packet of pamphlets out from its hiding place in the rafters.

He snipped the binding threads on the Sefer and spread the pages out across the table. Looking through his own printed work, he found one that would pass for the same paper and interleaved them, making a thicker chapbook of half Sefer Dumah and half women's prayers on a cheap woodblock. He stitched them together with three simple knots and folded the pages again to make them look as if they'd been handled together. Now anyone taking a quick look would mistake the magical text for what Kalman Senderovich would have called "women's nonsense."

Isser tucked this new hybrid creation back into his vest, blew out the lamp, and unblocked his door. He had ordinary criminal texts to sell while he thought about what to do with his stolen goods.

"I THINK WE SHOULD go back to Isser's room and look for this book," Adela said.

"But what about the body?" Sorel asked.

"If it's Kalman's daughter, it's nothing to do with Isser. Or anyway I don't think so." She thought for a moment, chewing her lip. "But then, he didn't tell me about Shulem-Yontif, either. Maybe he wouldn't have told me if he was planning to elope with some rich girl."

Sorel choked. "Elope? That's not what happened. And it might not be her anyway. I want to find out for certain."

"We'll split up, then. I'll go look for the book, and you find me once you're finished hearing the gossip."

Sorel hesitated to let Adela go alone, and then caught herself. It was Isser's argument again, trying to keep Adela out of trouble. Well, they were all in trouble already, and Sorel had already searched his apartment without finding anything.

"See you later, then," she said. "Watch out for—I don't know. Murderers and thieves and everything."

"You too," said Adela, rolling her eyes. "And behave yourself."

She walked off before Sorel could ask what that meant, taking the alleyway back toward Isser's neighborhood instead of the synagogue.

Sorel squeezed back past the rain barrel into the courtyard, just in time to see the crowd part for a man on horseback with a neatly trimmed red beard and a velvet cap.

Kalman Senderovich.

She stopped in her tracks, casting about for somewhere to hide without blocking her own view. After a moment she realized trying to hide would only make her more visible. He wasn't looking in her direction at all.

Behind him, she saw their coach and a flock of Hasidim helping the rebbe get down so he could hobble across the courtyard. People made way for him and her father as if they were kings. With the rebbe was a gentile who must have been an official of some kind, looking impatient at the old man's pace.

The whispers of the crowd had turned urgent. Kalman being here lent weight to the assertion that it was his daughter who'd been found.

She had to get a look at the body. While everyone was craning their necks to get a look at the rebbe and straining their ears to hear his conversation with the impatient gentile, she turned back to the alley and slipped out of the courtyard. The mikveh complex was in the street behind, with the hekdesh, the home for wanderers, and the mortuary. But she couldn't just walk in—the women from the chevra kadisha would be there. Unless.

She stopped, thinking. Could she pass for a maidservant? Pretend she was her own nanny come to look at the girl from the river, to see if it were really Sorel Kalmans? She'd need to be quick. While the men were still talking.

She cast her eyes around at the strings of laundry. There— an old-fashioned peasant's dress, certainly too big for her, and not fine enough quality to really meet Kalman's approval, but the city women might not know that. She tucked her coat and satchel behind the rain barrel and pulled the damp dress over her head. She grabbed a scarf from another line to wrap her hair as she hurried through the alley and turned toward the hekdesh. When she looked at herself in a grimy shop window she looked passable and certainly panicked enough to be a maidservant looking for her dead mistress.

There was a male bathhouse attendant standing outside, smoking a cigarette. Sorel ran up to him and fluttered her hands, trying to distract him from looking at her too closely.

"Is this the hekdesh? Is this where they brought that poor drowned girl, God forbid?" She tried to imitate the tone of the sort of person her father referred to scornfully as poor village Jews, even though most of the people he'd turned the epithet on lived in the city.

"That's right," said the attendant, looking at her askance. "Why?"

"I've just come with Kalman Senderovich from his estate! They said it was his daughter, drowned, may it not be so! He and the rebbe, may he live, are at the synagogue, but he sent me ahead to see the—to see her! May it not be so!"

She wrung her hands, for dramatic effect. The attendant looked distinctly uncomfortable.

"All right, all right," he said. "I'm not supposed to let just anyone in, you understand? There are liars and gossips in this town. How do I know you're really from Kalman's estate, huh?"

Sorel wished she'd thought to have a coin in her hand to bribe him with. The stocking with her money in it was tucked into her trouser pocket, and she couldn't very well hike up her skirts to get at it now. She wracked her brain.

"Kalman's daughter," she said. "Can I tell you what Kalman's daughter looks like? And if it isn't her then you don't have to let me in at all! Did you see the body?"

"No," he said, "but I can ask Penina, if you describe her."

He jerked his head toward the doorway, indicating that Penina was inside.

"All right." Sorel glanced around, expecting her father to come around the corner at any moment and ruin her charade. "All right. Kalman's daughter is a maiden, about seventeen years old, tall. Not so well built. Skinny, if you forgive me for saying. A redhead, with brown eyes. She's taller than you! That's not so usual for a girl, don't you think?"

She hoped he wouldn't think too hard about the fact that, had she not been hunching her shoulders and occasionally lifting her hands to her face to hide imaginary tears, she too would have been taller than he was. He didn't seem to notice, thankfully, stubbing out his cigarette on the brick wall and tucking it behind his ear before he went inside.

Sorel waited, heart pounding, for what felt like half an hour before he came back.

"All right," he said. "You can go in and take a look." Then, belatedly, "May her memory be a blessing."

Sorel had thought he'd come back and tell her there was no need to see the body at all, that it was clearly someone else. She stared at him for a moment in astonishment.

"Penina says come in and take a look," said the attendant. "It's what you came for, isn't it?"

"Yes! Yes, thank you, thank you." She hurried past him and slammed the door behind her. What the hell?

There was lamplight coming from a door on the right of the entryway. She followed it to a room where two women were sitting at a card table, knitting and looking not particularly bothered by the third presence in the room, a figure stretched out under a blanket on another table.

One of the women rose to her feet when she saw Sorel. "You're Kalman's maidservant?"

"That's right." Her voice was genuinely shaking now. She hadn't thought this through. She'd never seen a body! What was she thinking? It couldn't possibly be hers, so what use was knowing whose it was?

But Penina was already leading her gently by the elbow to the side of the table.

"She hadn't been in the water long, poor thing," she said, drawing back the blanket. "Is it her?"

Sorel didn't answer. She couldn't.

It was her.

SHE HAD EXPECTED something fresh from the river—a rusalka with weeds tangled in her hair, smelling of mud. But, of course, the women of the chevra kadisha had washed her. Sorel imagined them whispering prayers as they gently combed the knots from her hair. They might not have finished the taharah, since they didn't have a name for the body. She certainly wasn't dressed for burial. But someone had loosely braided her damp hair, without tying it off at the end, and laid it over her shoulder, as if she were sleeping.

It was her own face. She'd seen it in the mirror, she'd seen it in her dreams with Isser wearing it. When she touched the girl's cheek, it was cool and waxy, like a doll's face. It couldn't be real. How could it be?

"It's her, isn't it," said the woman at her shoulder. Penina, presumably. "May her memory be a blessing."

"It's Soreh bat Batsheva," Sorel said, her voice faraway in her ears. How had they not looked at her when she came in and instantly seen that it was the same face? Except neither of the women were really looking at her at all. Penina was looking at the body, and the other was looking at her knitting, squinting in the candlelight.

"I have to—" Sorel burst out, in a real sob. "I have to—"

Penina stepped back, giving her space, and she ran for the door. Only there was the sound of talking outside, men's voices, loud in the street. She couldn't go that way; she'd walk straight into her father's arms, and that was the last place she wanted to be when she was in a panic.

She dashed down the hall in the other direction. There would be a back door, to bring the coal in for the fires. She told herself so firmly, as if the words could make it true. And sure enough, she found a door that opened to a set of steps leading into a cellar that was stifling with trapped heat from the boiler in one corner. Here she tore off the stolen headscarf and dress, and kicked them behind a pile of kindling. Her hands were shaking so badly she almost couldn't get the door to the alley unlatched. Finally, it swung open and she was running full-tilt away from the bathhouse complex.

She only caught herself at the sound of a dog barking up ahead, a deep booming bark that froze her in her tracks. It sounded like the same dog—the damn werewolf, or whatever it was Yoshke had called it. She pressed herself against a wall, waiting, but no dog appeared, and the bark was not repeated.

When she got herself under control, she remembered that she'd left her satchel by the Great Synagogue, under the rain barrel. She'd have to go back and get it.

Go and get the bag and coat, then find Adela. She took a deep breath and looked around, finding her bearings. She needed to be practical. One foot in front of the next.

She had to have imagined the face under the sheet. Her eyes were playing tricks. She hadn't slept enough, she'd hit her head maybe, falling from the window at Pavlikov's club. She was going mad, and the corpse from the river was part of it but so was Isser; she'd imagined him entirely and she'd have to tell Adela so when she saw her again, and—

She stopped again, squeezed her eyes shut, and took another breath. No, it was just bad light and a girl who looked a bit like her and her own fear. She hadn't even really looked, had she? She'd had half her mind on listening for her father and the rebbe to come in and ruin her scheme.

The courtyard of the Great Synagogue was emptying out when she got there. People had gotten bored of waiting or her father had told them to go away or they had more important business. She didn't see Shulem-Yontif anywhere.

Her things were just where she'd left them. She pulled the coat on and checked the pockets for the reassuring weight of the knife, though she had no immediate use for it. No one was chasing her, not even the dog. If the dog actually existed.

The dog has to exist, she told herself. *Because if it doesn't, I tore those men apart with my teeth.*

She would remember doing that.

Probably.

AFTER SEVERAL WRONG TURNS, Sorel realized the problem with telling Adela to meet at Isser's apartment. She didn't remember the way, and all the streets looked the same, houses leaning like crooked teeth and alleys full of scrap wood and garbage. The gnawing hunger had returned as her panic drained away, so she finally gave up on trying to regain her bearings and sat in front of a kosher tavern like the one Sam had taken her to days before.

She drank a mug of strong scalding tea and ate bagels with herring. The gossips all around her were talking about how Kalman Senderovich's daughter had been pulled from the river, which meant that the wedding was cursed, which meant that the rebbe was cursed, which meant that Esrog was cursed.

She even heard the story about the three-eyed goat again. There was some disagreement on where the third eye had been located. Sorel leaned her chin in her hand and picked apart her second bagel.

"Of course everyone knows he's a miracle worker," a man was saying at the table next to her. "They say when he was young, he stopped a drought that had gone on so long that even the tsar himself sent a purse to the rebbe in thanks."

"He healed my cousin's sister-in-law's fever," said another man. "He gave her some holy names, and it just went away. She would have died otherwise."

"He stops the river from flooding the lower city every single year," someone else added.

"Then if someone's put the evil eye on him, should we look out for rain?"

Everyone, Sorel included, glanced up at the sky. It did look rather gloomy, but Sorel felt foolish for checking. She'd never believed in the rebbe's miracles, largely because her father, despite his lack of superstition, was so careful never to discount them. He didn't like the Hasidim, he found them unruly. But he liked having his own personal Baal-Shem.

"We should worry who's got the kind of sorcery that can put the evil eye on a tzadik like that to begin with," said the man whose relative had been healed of her fever.

"Someone didn't like the thought of there being one united Esroger Jewish community," said another, lowering his voice conspiratorially and glancing around. "If the Hasidim and the kahal agree with each other, there's more of us than there are of the goyim. Don't you think Kalman Senderovich knows that? A Jew doesn't get rich by being stupid. When the Hasidim first came the kahal wanted to be rid of them. Once it was clear they're not leaving, he changed his tune."

"I don't think it speaks well of the rebbe," said one of the men, irritable. "Making nice with a man like that."

"A tzadik is always forgiving! Of course he would make nice with Kalman. It's the right thing—for the Jews, for all of us."

Sorel chewed her bagel slowly, no longer because she was hungry, but so she had an excuse to keep listening. She'd never liked the rebbe because he was her prospective father-in-law. She'd always vaguely assumed his followers were ignorant, superstitious village Jews—which she now realized was her father talking. These men believed in the rebbe, even though they weren't dressed as Hasidim, and judging by the neighboring shops, these men were city artisans. They liked the rebbe more than they liked her father, in fact they hated her father. This didn't surprise her. Kalman wasn't easy to like, and he oversaw the collection of taxes for the Jewish community. No one liked that, even if most of the money went to fixing synagogues and supporting orphans and whatnot. The rebbe, as far as she knew, did nothing but perform miracles.

It had never occurred to her that the rebbe might be working with her father out of something more complicated than the friendship between two old men who each ruled his own kingdom. Her father talked of the rebbe behind his back in ways that weren't always glowing, but she'd assumed, somehow, that the simple miracle worker wouldn't have an ulterior motive.

"Alter!" A voice interrupted her thoughts, and she looked around, annoyed at the interruption, to see Sam waving cheerfully from down the street. He jogged over and sat across from her without being invited. "I'm glad I found you. I worried you and Adela had been swallowed up, God forbid, by demons."

"No," said Sorel. "And you? Did you get swallowed up by demons?"

"No. I ran when some wild maniac goy pulled a gun, and then I spent the night at the Gravediggers' Synagogue because I left my things there." He shrugged a shoulder to indicate his peddler's pack. "Have you heard?"

"That they really did pull Kalman Senderovich's daughter from the river?" she said. "The whole city's heard."

"They'll be burying her as soon as the goyim are done with their city inquest," said Sam quite cheerfully, taking a piece of bagel off Sorel's plate. He whispered the blessing for bread and popped it into his mouth. "It was the talk of the Gravediggers' minyan, as you can imagine. Taking her back to Kalman's estate, I think."

"He doesn't mix with ordinary people," said Sorel bitterly. They were taking a body back to the estate, to bury next to her mother. A body that she couldn't even blame her father for thinking was hers. She'd thought the same.

"Half the city thinks it's Tisheb'ov," said Sam, who evidently didn't agree, as he was stealing another piece of Sorel's bagel. "As if this girl were the Messiah, pardon the comparison."

Sorel made a face. She certainly hadn't felt like a messiah. More like a doll, like the cold waxen figure she'd touched in the mikveh.

It occurred to her, suddenly, that if Soreh Kalmans was dead and buried, Sorel herself was no longer missing. No one would be looking for her. They had found her.

Her heart skipped in her chest. A strange feeling, incongruous against the memory of her own placid, drowned face in the candlelight. The feeling of freedom.

Sorel Kalmans was dead. She could be whoever she wanted. Now no one would be looking at her face and measuring it against the description of a missing girl.

She tried to swallow the feeling, to keep it from showing on her face. She grabbed the plate of bagels and yanked it back to her side of the table, away from Sam. "Are you paying for those?"

He gave her a crooked grin and dug in his pocket. "You're a strict one, Isser-Alter."

"You're superstitious," Sorel said thoughtfully.

"And?" said Sam.

"What I mean is, you know the sorts of things a rational Jew would call bobe-mayses."

He laughed. "I suppose."

"Is there a way to speak to a ghost? Say, if you found a body and you didn't know whose it was—could you ask the soul, somehow?"

She expected mockery, but Sam gave it some serious thought. "Did you get a message from someone's ghost when you slept in the graveyard?"

"No. I'm just wondering. Is that how you'd do it?"

"The rabbis disagree," said Sam. "On whether a ghost can tell you anything at all. But isn't the cemetery where you'd go, in that situation?"

"Ugh!" Sorel looked away dismissively. "Just answer with an answer or tell me you don't know it."

"You didn't need to speak to Kalman's daughter, did you?" Sam asked. "Don't tell me you planned to elope with her."

"Why assume she drowned because she was trying to elope?" Sorel snapped. "Even Adela considered it! Why not assume she was running away alone? Maybe she had a life to go to."

Sam shrugged. "I heard a rumor that she was going to the nuns. They can't make you marry a Jew if you've converted— some girls do it."

"Absolutely not."

"You did know her, then." He gave her a sympathetic look. "I'm sorry."

Sorel frowned, hunching her shoulders, and shredded the bagel in her hands. "Not that well. Her father didn't really let her know anyone."

There was silence for a minute, Sam letting her feel her false grief for the lost bride. His consideration annoyed her. She wished he would have said something irritating, so she could snap at him again.

"If I did need to speak to her," she said at last, "you'd say to go to her grave?"

"I suppose so," said Sam. "Or there are charms for dreams, if you can't go to the grave. If you're searching for someone whose gravesite you don't know."

He slid his pack off his back as he spoke.

"You sell those charms, don't you?" said Sorel.

"Of course I do. But for you, there's no charge." He dug in the pack and slid a little pouch across the table to her. "It's kosher. Only the names of angels. No kind of goyish magic."

"I don't care," said Sorel frankly. "And I can pay for it. How do I use it?"

"Put it under your pillow when you sleep. Simple enough."

She put the charm in her pocket. She wasn't sure she'd use it—she wasn't even sure what use she thought it would be, if it was even real. But she liked having it, just in case. Maybe she could find Isser with it.

"What happened to Adela?" Sam asked, breaking her concentration. Glad of the change of subject, she explained Adela's plan to search Isser's room again, without mentioning Shulem-Yontif specifically. She was getting used to the idea of secrets.

"And we learned that he had a book," she said. "Something called Sefer Dumah. Speaking of angels."

Sam's eyebrows shot up. "What? Where did you learn that?"

"From someone who knew him." She had after all promised not to tell anyone it was Shulem-Yontif who gave it to him.

She lowered her voice and leaned closer to Sam. "He stole it from the rebbe. The Esroger tzadik. And now it's missing along with Isser."

"God forbid the wrong person should have it," said Sam. "That's a very holy book, a secret book. And it's dangerous. Do you know the story of the four who entered Paradise?"

Sorel shook her head.

"There were four Sages who entered Paradise. One died, one went mad, one became a heretic, and only Rabbi Akiva returned unharmed. There are certain kinds of knowledge it isn't safe to seek."

"Unless you're Rabbi Akiva," said Sorel.

"Yes, well, who would dare assume he's Rabbi Akiva?"

Sorel thought about it. She didn't have the impression that Isser was particularly learned in Hebrew, and she didn't think he was particularly arrogant, either. But she did suspect he was enough like herself that he wouldn't have believed a book could hold that kind of danger. Not from simply reading it. "Can a book be as powerful as entering Paradise? Surely not."

"Paradise is a book," said Sam. "It's a place built of the same Hebrew letters that built the world. No book a human hand could write contains all of Paradise, but a book that captures even one chapter of it can change the world. And Sefer Dumah isn't just any book; it was written by an angel, with its own hand."

"Hm." It sounded fanciful. But if other people believed it, they might kill over it. Isser may have died because he had it. In which case, whoever had the book was the person who'd killed him. "I don't suppose you've got an amulet for finding lost books?"

"When a village housewife has a priceless Kabbalistic text, she keeps track of where she left it," said Sam dryly.

CHAPTER

14

THEY FOUND ADELA sitting on the steps up to Isser's room, reading one of the books in German that had been scattered by the searchers.

"His tfillin case is missing," she said. "You two didn't see it, did you? It's embroidered with foxes, two foxes holding a scroll."

Sorel shook her head and looked at Sam. He shrugged.

"I didn't think to look for them," he said. "He didn't strike me as one who prays daily."

"He's not," Adela agreed. "But they were his father's, and his mother made the case—may their memories be a blessing. Did you speak to anyone at the print shop?"

Again, they shook their heads. Adela sighed, as if to say *I have to do everything myself.* "We should at least ask them if they know who broke in. Come on."

The print shop was quiet, not closed but conducting business discreetly for the Christian sabbath. An older man with a beard and spectacles was checking over the presses while a couple of apprentices with short sidelocks cleaned type at a table under the window. The old man gave the three a suspicious look as they walked in the room. He came out from between the presses to greet them, but he had a piece of metal in his hand, some piece of the machines that he held casually, as if by chance, but kept in their sight. The apprentices paused with their cleaning rags in hand, staring.

"You need something?" the printer asked, eyeing each of them in turn. Sorel checked her pocket for her knife and then wondered if that made her look more suspicious.

"We're looking for Isser Jacobs," said Adela.

The old man tightened his grip on the metal rod. Adela and Sam both held up their hands immediately, Sorel following their example a second later.

"What do you want him for?" said the printer, glaring. He wasn't a particularly big man, an older Jew who would look right at home behind a volume of Mishnah in the bet midrash, but his eyes were fierce. Sorel heard the apprentices shifting in their seats and glanced around to see them tensed, ready to leap up.

"We don't want any trouble," said Sam coolly.

"You'd better not," said the old man. "We've had enough of it already. You with that apostate bastard Yoshke? I've nothing more to say to him."

Yoshke again. "We're not with him," said Sorel. "We don't like him either."

At that the old man, and his apprentices, relaxed a little, but he didn't put down his cudgel. "What, then?"

"We're trying to figure out who's been making trouble for Isser," said Adela. "Someone trashed his rooms, and they've taken some things—a book."

"I don't know about that," said the printer. "All we know is no one's seen Isser since, what?"

He looked around at his apprentices, who exchanged looks.

"At least last Shabbat," one of them said.

"He was going to meet Shulem-Yontif," said the other. "He told me. You know Isser, only comes to minyan when he wants something. We were leaving after prayers and he said he'd see me in the morning, he was off to the river. But he never showed up."

"What did he want at minyan?" Adela asked. "We're trying to find out what happened. We think he's tangled up in something bad."

The apprentices and the printer all looked at each other again, a knowing look.

"Everyone knows Isser's trouble, missy," said the printer. "You'd do better to keep out of it, yourself."

Adela crossed her arms over her chest, planting her feet in a stubborn posture as if she expected him to try to push her out of his shop. Sorel unconsciously mirrored her. "That doesn't answer my question."

"What did he want at minyan?" said the apprentice who'd seen Isser last, while shrugging elaborately. "Talk, talk, talk. I don't know. It was Shacharit, I was half asleep."

"Well, who else goes to minyan to talk?" Sorel demanded. "Yoshke? You don't look like you'd be with the Hasidim."

The boy shook his head. "Nah. I think God would strike Yoshke down if he tried to touch a siddur. I don't know, some old man." He glanced at the printer and grinned. "Not as old as my father."

"And who else was in the minyan?" said Sam. "Maybe they know who it was."

"You're thinking someone from the paper trades' shul jumped Isser in an alley?" the printer said, and shook his head. "No. We work together."

"There was someone last Shabbat," said the other apprentice, who'd been quiet until now. "Some out-of-towner, wasn't it?"

"Right." The other apprentice's eyes lit up. "Nice boots, he had."

"Light hair," said his companion. Sorel didn't think they were brothers—they didn't look alike—but they clearly worked well together. She felt a stab of jealousy at their easy friendship.

"Light hair with a beard," said the talkative one, and both laughed. "Well, who doesn't have a beard?"

Neither of them, and neither Sam nor Sorel—but it was a fair point.

"Someone might know what he was in town for," said the printer reluctantly. He clearly didn't like the idea of bringing Isser's trouble to his brother artisans, but Sorel thought he also wanted the three of them out of his shop—and perhaps out of this conversation with his son. "We didn't talk business on Shabbat, of course. But someone might have brought him because he was talking business with them when it wasn't Shabbat. Try Shimen the papermaker. His shop's two streets that way, on the river."

He pointed with his improvised cudgel.

"Before we go," said Adela, "you don't have any of Isser's books, do you? He didn't leave any in the shop?"

The printer sighed and looked over at his son again.

"What kind of books?" said the son, with a credible lack of shiftiness.

"Any," said Adela. "Can I see?"

"We've got a little library." The boy got up, dropping his cleaning rag on top of his friend's, and beckoned them to follow. The library was in a back room that also served as a kitchen, with a door that opened into the alley. It was just a

THE FORBIDDEN BOOK

single shelf, an odd collection of mostly battered secular texts in Russian, with a few Yiddish pamphlets.

"Are these all censor-approved?" Adela asked.

"Of course!" said the printer's apprentice. "Otherwise, it wouldn't be legal to have them, would it?"

He winked at her.

"You're the translator, aren't you?" he added, before she could ask anything else. "Isser told me it was a girl. Secretly, of course. Here, I'll show you."

He went to the other side of the room and lifted the lid off the kindling bin by the stove. There was a box tucked into the kindling, which he opened to show them a stack of more Yiddish pamphlets—Sorel thought she recognized one of them as the one Sam had shown her to prove he was liable for the same criminal activities as Isser.

"Can I take a look?" Adela asked, already reaching for the box.

"It's just politics in there," said the apprentice, though he handed it to her anyway. "If you're his translator I'm sure you've already seen them."

Adela flipped through the pamphlets without responding. Evidently she didn't find anything. She looked up at Sam and Sorel and shook her head as she tucked them back in their box.

"Mottel!" the printer shouted from the front of the shop.

"That's time for me to get back to work," said the apprentice. He put the box back in amongst the kindling, scattered a few bits of bark over it, and shut the bin. "You remember where Shimen the papermaker is?"

"We'll find him," said Sam, although Sorel had in fact already forgotten the directions.

"Thank you," said Adela.

Mottel gave her another wink. Was he flirting? Sorel sighed inwardly. Poor Adela, she couldn't talk to anyone without them reminding her she was a woman. It must be such tedium to be pretty.

The printer stood in the door, cudgel still in hand, watching them until they turned off his street. Sorel could feel his eyes on the back of her neck.

"I think he knows something more than he told us," she said after the third time she looked back to find him still glaring.

"He does," Sam agreed. "But maybe Shimen the papermaker knows even more."

"Or Shulem-Yontif," said Adela. "Did you catch that, Alter? He said Isser went to see Shulem-Yontif and never came back."

"Shulem-Yontif couldn't kill somebody," Sorel objected. It wasn't that she wanted to defend her fiancé, so much. She just couldn't imagine it. He'd been sobbing in pieces just because she—her double, whom he had scarcely spoken to—was dead. And Isser had been his friend. If Shulem-Yontif had been involved in Isser's death, his soul would have fled his body.

"Maybe, maybe not," said Adela. "Maybe he was the bait in a trap."

Sorel didn't have any argument against that.

CHAPTER
15

MINYAN AT THE PAPERMAKERS' SHUL was always crowded.
Though the attendees were not worthy of praying in the Great
Synagogue itself, they considered themselves second only to
that honorable congregation, as the business of paper—in all
stages of its life from pulp and rag to printed book—had long
been Esrog's most prosperous industry. The older men talked
a lot about how things had been better before Isser was born,
when the censors were less strict and the road that passed by
Esrog better traveled, but Isser only halfway believed any of
it. Their crown prince of a shul was made of wood and plas-
ter, and its floors creaked and snapped like gunshots through-
out the services, making it difficult to keep one's place.

He was used to being accosted outside the shul by Kalman
Senderovich's messengers—Ostap, usually. He expected to

see the other boy today, lurking outside, and was surprised when he didn't.

Instead, he found the messenger waiting inside, head down over a siddur like all the others. It was Kalman himself, and Isser's heart sank into his boots. He hadn't expected Kalman to actually answer his summons. He didn't feel ready to talk to him.

Reluctantly, he slid into the bench at Kalman's elbow, mouthing the blessings while he searched for the right place in the prayer book. Kalman glanced sideways at him and gave a curt nod of acknowledgement. That was all. He was going to make Isser wait until the conclusion of the service. Isser felt himself sweating from more than the stuffy air of the crowded shul.

When services ended and the men gathered around the stove for gossip and snifters of vodka, Kalman stepped aside into the alcove that hid the women's gallery stairs, and Isser tucked himself into the shadows beside him.

"Do you have the book?" Kalman said, without even a greeting.

"I have questions," said Isser. "Before I turn that thing over to you and make an enemy of the rebbe for my life. Why is this worth risking your daughter's engagement for? You can't really believe it's magic."

His hands were clammy. He stuffed them in his pockets so as not to show his nerves. Kalman was giving him the slightly pitying look he always used when Isser talked back to him.

"I think you know the book is genuine," Kalman said. "I would not waste my time for a bit of fakery. And for all his flaws, neither would Nachum-Eydl. I ask you again, have you brought it?"

"Why?" Isser repeated stubbornly. "I looked into it. The old women say the first rebbe used that book to keep the Angel of Death off our backs somehow. Can't be so much protection, people die in Esrog all the time. But it's got to do something, or you wouldn't care if he had it. Right? So what is it doing, really?"

"Who have you been talking to?" Kalman demanded. He moved closer in the small space, cornering Isser against the door. "You were to keep this business completely secret."

"I didn't tell anyone I had it," Isser whispered. "I'm not an idiot. It's just gossip. No one knows about it."

"The rebbe's protection is genuine," Kalman said, relenting a little and taking half a step back. "But flawed. The contract prevents certain kinds of change from reaching the city. In the shelter of the rebbe's magic, Esrog stagnates. You're young, perhaps you haven't seen it. But we were a gem once, this city. Once, you would not have questioned that the angels held us in favor. Now our streets are littered with beggars, trade flows miles to the east along the railroad, and the people turn to desperate superstition instead of taking action."

"So?" Isser prompted, when the lumber merchant trailed off into a contemplative silence. "What is it you want the book for?"

"The world has changed," said Kalman. "We must change. I intend to destroy it."

"But you just said it protects us."

Kalman shook his head slightly. "Israel, you understand the modern world. I know you do. Those pamphlets you peddle— Jewish Emancipation, accusations against the kahal, encouraging women to read. You understand that those ideas are dangerous. You understand the risk, but you're clever. You see that the danger is necessary. I don't agree with those sentimental stories about overturning society and whatnot, but I appreciate your conviction. You're a clever young man. That's why I entrusted this task to you."

"What happens when you destroy it, though? How do we know it doesn't call down a disaster on our heads? It's the Book of the Angel of Death. Do Angels of Death listen to reason?"

"It is a risk," Kalman agreed. "A risk balanced against a certainty. If Esrog doesn't change, we will all be lost. I am trusting you with this. You could destroy me. Take this to the rebbe, and it's all over—my daughter's wedding, my place on the council. And he would destroy Esrog along with me."

Isser hesitated, biting his thumbnail.

"I buried your mother," Kalman said, leaning closer and laying a gentle hand on Isser's shoulder. "I paid for her funeral. I saw to it that when Nachum-Eydl needed someone to take his son's place in the secular school, it was you who received an education. You'd be up to your ankles in the muck down in the river bottom still, and you'd never have had a single thought about politics without me. Now they're taking my daughter. You're the closest to a son that I have—my Kaddish. I need you to help me with this."

"Why not just talk to the rebbe?" Isser murmured.

"Do you think I haven't? That I haven't argued over this with him? He insists that we must stand together."

His eyes were dark and intense. He truly believed what he was saying.

But Kalman always believed his own words.

I'm not your Kaddish, Isser thought.

"It's here," he said, taking the pamphlet from his vest pocket. "I only wanted to hear . . . to know that you had a plan for it."

Ostap was waiting for Kalman on the street outside, and Isser felt his eyes on the back of his neck, cold as ice, until he turned the corner into the alley. Guilt, stalking him like a hunting dog.

He wished he hadn't given up his knife.

CHAPTER

16

SHIMEN THE PAPERMAKER did not know more than the printer, or else he was even better at hiding it. They spent the rest of the day circling the printers' district, being sent from one person to the next with barely more than the repeated warning not to get tangled up in Isser's trouble. Adela and Sam seemed to have endless stamina for being on their feet, but Sorel couldn't take it in the end and demanded they stop for a rest and something to eat just before sunset.

She was starting to worry about the decreasing weight of the sock holding her coins, but there was nothing to be done about it—she couldn't think and she couldn't walk without food in her. When they passed a kosher house serving massive plates of fried potatoes and herring, Sorel planted her feet and refused to go farther.

"Either they're all in on it together, or nobody actually knows anything anyway," she said, when Adela looked reluctant to give up the chase. "Come on, you have to eat."

"My family are going to know something's wrong by now," said Adela, aggravated. "I should be going back to Kuritsev."

Sam, always easygoing, was already moving to the tavern door. "Alter's right. Come on. No one's talking."

Adela heaved a sigh and followed them inside. They found a spot in a corner to sit, and Sorel paid for two plates of potatoes. Adela had claimed that she wasn't hungry, but once the food was in front of her she started eating with almost as much enthusiasm as Sorel, while Sam watched them both with an expression of benign amusement.

"I just want to find him," said Adela. "Or find his book, or—I just want to know what he was doing. We aren't supposed to have secrets from each other."

She gave Sorel a hungry look as she spoke, which made Sorel's heart flip over uneasily. It wasn't that the look was unwelcome, actually she quite liked the idea of Adela looking at her with such intensity. But she wanted it to be her Adela was seeing. She knew Adela's stare was for Isser, and he wasn't even there.

"I don't know the answer to that," she said reluctantly. It felt wrong to lie, though the temptation was there. Just to make Adela keep looking at her. She couldn't think of how to phrase a lie without alerting Sam to the fact that she was either dybbuk-ridden or a madman, anyway.

"We've talked to criminals, and we've talked to honest tradesmen," said Sam. "Who's left?"

"Women?" said Sorel.

Sam shrugged. Adela chewed her lip, looking thoughtful.

"He sold pamphlets in the mother tongue," said Sam. "He could be selling them to mothers, no?"

He had a point, but Sorel didn't like it. She stuffed her mouth full of potatoes so she'd have an excuse for not speaking for a moment. The truth was she still worried that any women she spoke to would see through her, see through Alter—even though Adela hadn't. And how did one start a conversation with a woman, anyway? Where did you even find them?

"I meant the Hasidim, though," said Sam. "Didn't Yoshke mention something?"

"The one Yoshke told us about was Shulem-Yontif, who they mentioned at the printers too," said Adela.

"But he's no good," said Sorel. "We talked to him already. And he's a damp noodle."

Sam looked between them, a silent request for more details. Adela was scowling in Sorel's direction.

"He is a damp noodle, but that doesn't mean he's not involved," she insisted. "What is it with you, Alter? Every time someone mentions a specific name you say it can't be him.

Can't be Kalman the lumber merchant—when everyone knows Kalman and everyone knows he's ruthless. Can't be Shulem-Yontif either."

"But you saw him," said Sorel.

"I saw someone frightened," said Adela. "Frightened doesn't mean not guilty. And he's a hasid who's been reading books he isn't supposed to. Don't you think we shouldn't rule out the one person we know is hiding something?"

"Everyone we've talked to is hiding something!" Sorel exclaimed. "Yoshke has things to hide, and no one likes him, you said yourself he's suspicious. As well as those goyim who almost shot us!"

"We know something now that we didn't know when we talked to Shulem-Yontif," Adela said, lowering her voice deliberately. "We know he was the last to see Isser."

"We don't," said Sorel stubbornly. "All we know is Isser said he was going to see him. We don't know that Isser made it to the meeting."

Sam was watching both of their faces with an expression of mild confusion. "Who is Shulem-Yontif?"

Sorel stabbed a potato with her fork. "He's the hasid Yoshke mentioned, and we found out Isser was teaching him Russian."

"And he's Kalman's son-in-law," said Adela. "Except also, he isn't actually, because the bride drowned in the river before they could be married. So he's involved in two deaths."

"Do you know Isser is dead, God forbid?" said Sam mildly.

"It seems silly to assume he isn't," said Adela.

"We don't know Shulem-Yontif had anything to do with the drowning either," said Sorel. "I mean she just drowned. It doesn't even have to be murder."

Adela looked exasperated. "Be reasonable, Alter."

It was a tall order, when nothing that had happened for the last week or more had been reasonable. But it seemed like a bad idea to keep fighting with Adela in public, so she jammed her mouth full of food once again and refused to speak. They ate the rest of their meal in huffy silence.

THEY HAD INTENDED to spend the night in Isser's room again, but when they turned into his street they found it tense with the unmistakable air of a neighborhood where something was amiss. Skin crawling, Sorel withdrew the knife from her pocket and held it with both hands in front of her as they made their way quietly between the darkened houses. Nearer the courtyard, there were a handful of men standing in their own doorways, watching the street. They could have possibly just been getting some air, maybe sharing a bit of gossip, but they were too alert. Their eyes followed Sorel and the others as they approached the courtyard, then one of the men spoke up.

"Wouldn't go back there if you're Isser's friends."

"You're the ones asking about him, aren't you?" said the man in the next door over. "Watch your backs. Someone got a sniff of you, I'll bet. They're turning over his rooms again."

"Who is?" Sorel asked. All that tramping around the city and the people they'd been searching for were here all along? And the neighbors knew it? She made herself lower the knife so it wouldn't appear she was threatening him.

"Some hooligans. Best stay out of it, lad."

Sorel, Sam, and Adela retreated to the next alley to deliberate. They all agreed that one of them should look and see if they recognized any of the so-called hooligans, but they disagreed on who it should be. Neither Sorel nor Adela was willing to back down, and at last Sam heaved a sigh and suggested they both go together.

"Only don't kill each other on the way," he said. "I'll watch your backs, how's that? And don't confront them, please."

"Not if we're outnumbered, anyway," said Sorel.

"Not at all," said Sam, but with a tone of resignation.

Sorel and Adela cut through the alley to the other side of the courtyard, where they could approach Isser's rooms from what would hopefully be an unexpected angle: another alleyway that was barely more than a crack between two walls, with ditch water running along it. It smelled terrible, but it afforded them a shadowy place to peer out into the courtyard and watch the stairs without making themselves obvious.

There was a man at the bottom of the stairs, standing in a guard's stance but with an air of impatience. Not just a guard's stance, Sorel realized when lamplight from an open window glinted off his buttons—he was a city guard. She felt suddenly sick, remembering her escape, and had to step back and lean for a moment against the wall.

Adela, still watching, took in a sharp breath.

"Yoshke!" she hissed, waving to Sorel to join her at the mouth of the alley.

A group of men was coming down the stairs, a couple carrying lanterns. Yoshke was indeed one of them, and the others she thought were gentiles. They looked more like Pavlikov's comrades than like guardsmen, but the guardsman was clearly part of the group. They were engaged in a discussion Sorel and Adela were too far away to hear—Yoshke gesticulating as if he were trying to get a point across, the other men shaking their heads—and then the group broke up. The gentiles left Yoshke alone by the well, head down.

"Let's get him," Sorel whispered in Adela's ear. "Two of us, one of him."

She was worried that after their argument Adela wouldn't go along with it, but Adela nodded and stepped forward. Sorel drew the knife and leapt after her, automatically putting herself between Yoshke and the exit to the main street. Yoshke looked up and jumped sideways, trying to run, but not fast enough—Adela caught him by the back of the collar and Sorel planted herself, and her knife, in front of him.

"So!" she said. "You're not in league with Pavlikov, is it? You don't have anything to do with whatever's going on between him and Isser? You don't know what Isser's been up to or where he's gone? Have I got all that right?"

Yoshke was looking at the knife. When he showed no sign of trying to wrench himself out of her grip, Adela let go of his jacket and stepped back, but only far enough that she was closer to the well. Her hand hovered close to the handle of the heavy bucket that sat on top of the well cover.

"You left me with Pavlikov!" Yoshke said, holding up his hands. "They thought I'd set them up! I had to show them Isser's room to prove I'm not in league with you."

Sorel took a step closer to him, keeping the knife low, at gut level. There was a vicious satisfaction in it, being the one offering threats instead of responding to them. She felt a little of Isser's rage bubbling up again, the memory of the strength he'd used to turn over the table in Pavlikov's room. "It would be a terrible shame if you were lying to us, Yoshke. After you brought us into danger."

"It wasn't dangerous!" Yoshke exclaimed. "Not until you started acting crazy. Who the hell are you, anyway? What was that? How did you know about—" He looked around, as if checking for eavesdroppers. "How do you know Pavlikov's business? You're not even from Esrog; no one's seen you before."

"You think I'd share that information with you?" said Sorel. "What did you think you'd find in Isser's rooms?"

"I hoped I'd find Isser," said Yoshke, backing away from her a step. "But someone's turned the place over. Listen, Pavlikov wants your head. I don't know what you did to him, but he wants your beitzim in a pickle jar."

"Thanks for the warning," said Adela. "But it isn't exactly a surprise."

"He's been raving about it all night," said Yoshke. "If I were you, I'd get out of the city. Speedily."

"Not until we finish our business here," said Adela. "Were you looking for anything else in Isser's rooms?"

"What?" said Yoshke. "Like money? Everyone knows he doesn't have any. He's always feeding that old blind beggar woman or buying fish for alley cats or some other foolishness."

Adela looked at Sorel. Her eyes said "Is he lying?"

Sorel couldn't claim to be an expert, but he didn't seem to be. He was trying to make eye contact with her, for one. For another, he hadn't tried to run again, and he certainly could have.

"Look," said Yoshke. "I don't know anything more, all right? I showed those guys the rooms, they didn't find anything, and now they're spitting mad, and I'm getting out of here. I'm going back to Kuritsev, all right? So don't try to talk to me again. I never want to see you, ever," he added, throwing a hand in Sorel's direction. "You're a madman."

He tried to take a step to the side, but she and Adela mirrored the movement, keeping him cornered, Adela picking up the bucket in a smooth motion.

"Not so fast," said Sorel. "Do you know anything about a book called Sefer Dumah?"

Yoshke blinked at her. It was a very convincing impression of bafflement, if false. "I don't read Hebrew," he said shortly. "Now can I go?"

Sorel looked at Adela for guidance. Adela gave it a second's thought, then waved a hand. "All right, go then. But if I hear that you haven't left town after all, I'm letting Alter be as crazy as he likes."

Yoshke grimaced and slipped out from between them, walking briskly out of the courtyard as if he really wanted to run, but didn't want to compromise his dignity. Sorel put her knife away, a little reluctantly. Something in her wanted to chase after him and jump on his neck.

"He didn't know the room was already searched," said Adela. "And if Pavlikov needed Yoshke to show him where it was, that means it wasn't him that did it either."

"Do you think the neighbors know, after all?" Sorel asked. "They could have been bribed, or threatened. If it was city guards, like that one just now, they wouldn't want to talk about it, would they?"

"And if it was Jews, they might not have noticed," said Adela. "Who'd notice a Jew in a Jewish neighborhood?"

It was an unsatisfying conclusion. They stood there a moment longer, then Adela sighed and waved for Sorel to follow her back down the alley. They found Sam where they'd left him, sitting on his heels under the eaves of a house and chatting with the housewife about the weather.

"Pavlikov's men have been searching the apartment," Adela told him. "And it seems it wasn't them who did it the first time, either. They were upset that they hadn't found anything. We can't sleep there. Anyone could come back. I suppose we're lucky they didn't come back last night," she added, with a troubled glance in Sorel's direction.

Sorel had to agree. She'd been so deeply asleep, she might not have woken up if someone had.

To cover the unpleasant feeling, she returned Adela's look with a grin. "How do you feel about cemeteries?"

CHAPTER

17

THE FOREST IN SOREL'S dreams was moonlit and foggy, tendrils of mist creeping between the trees. She crept alongside them on her fox-feet, sniffing the air. Alongside the dark, earthy smell of the forest there was a strange perfume, compelling, drawing her onward. It reminded her of the parade through the streets in Kuritsev—the scent, maybe, that had clung to the ink-dark hair of that girl she had wanted to talk to before Isser interrupted her.

Grinning, she trotted after the scent. In the forest before, in her fox shape, she'd been afraid, feeling the dog on her trail. Now she was relaxed, feeling no hint of danger. In such an optimistic mood, she could appreciate the keenness of her own senses and the busy activity of a forest at night, with little creatures rustling in the litter on the ground and in the branches over her head. Her fox paws did not tire the way her human feet did, and felt their way easily along the broken ground, leaping over tree roots and skirting obstacles with such grace it was impossible not to enjoy.

Soon enough she came upon a stone wall with an iron gate. Here was the source of the perfume: a profusion of flowers that nearly obscured the stones of the wall. Roses she recognized. The flowering trees on either side of the gate, thick with pale pink, star-shaped clusters, she didn't know. The place looked abandoned, yet she felt a promise in it.

Sorel slipped beneath the rusted iron gate and trotted up the drive, over moss-covered cobbles displaced by frost heaves and the occasional sprouting bramble. The house, when it came into view, was even grander than her own father's estate. It rose four stories to a gabled roof that seemed to scrape the dark low-hanging clouds, the grey stone of the facade hung with more roses and ivy.

Sorel the Fox felt no compunctions about approaching the door, where a single lantern gave out a misty light that barely broke through the fog. She stood on her hind legs and clattered the knocker until the door opened.

Behind it was Isser, looking down at her. He was dressed as a footman from the last century in knee-breeches and stockings with his hair curled at his temples and a pair of spotless white gloves. Isser with his own face, this time. Fox-Sorel grinned and chattered at him.

He stepped back and opened the door wider to let her in but stopped her just past the threshold. Inside, the house was lit by the same wavering blue lights, leaving pools of shadow in every corner.

"I'd better take your coat," Isser said. "She won't want you in the house like that."

Sorel sat on her haunches and scratched her shoulder with a hind leg. *She who?*

"The lady you've come to see," said Isser, not making eye contact. "Have you got fleas?"

Maybe! Sorel laughed. *I don't know how to stop being a fox. You look all right as a footman. But what is this place?*

"It's a Gehinnom," said Isser. "Come on then, if you must be a fox, at least you can be a clean one. Please stop scratching."

Sorel gave her ears one last good scratch, just to spite him, and trotted after him to a hidden door that led to a servants' staircase.

You and I have a lot to talk about, Isser Jacobs, she said in her fox chatter. *What's this with Shulem-Yontif and stealing a book?*

"Shh," said Isser. "You shouldn't even be here, so don't go asking too many questions or you'll be stuck forever."

He opened another door, leading them into a bedroom where two small figures stood on either side of a steaming porcelain bathtub. They might have been children, or just child-sized. It was impossible to tell, as one had the head of a cat and the other the head of an owl, and both had the bare clawed feet of barnyard fowl. The owl-headed page was holding a stack of towels, and the other one a stack of folded clothing.

Sorel didn't wait to be invited to wash. The water looked so clean and warm, and somewhere under her fur she remembered she had human muscles that ached from running and walking and leaping out of windows. She put her paws up on the edge of the tub and launched herself in with a splash.

When her head came out of the water, she saw she was human again, and naked, as if the fox coat had simply melted off her. Isser handed her a bar of soap without looking at her, though she found she didn't mind his presence all that much. The little creature-servants goggled at her unashamedly, so she stared back. They too were dressed in last century's fashions, one in satin breeches and the other in a lace-edged pinafore, though Sorel didn't want to assume that meant the one was male and the other female.

"Where are we?" she asked Isser again, as she massaged the sweet-smelling soap into her hair. "I thought I was dreaming, but I've never smelled perfume in a dream before."

"You're not dreaming," Isser said. "It's real. You're just not in the world. Like I said, you shouldn't be here."

"Because I'm not dead, like you?"

He stared down, frowning at a spot on the floor rather than looking at her, and she wasn't sure if it was because she was naked, or because he didn't want to talk. She felt, in a remnant of the connection between them, the echo of a sullen reluctance.

"Yes," he said, after a grudging moment. "Because you're not dead, yet. And I'd rather you stayed that way."

She ducked her head under the water to rinse the soap out of her hair. Isser came forward and plucked a comb and a pair of scissors from the top of the stack of towels in the owl-page's arms and started to finger-comb her hair.

"You're in Agrat bat Machlat's country estate," he said. "Or anyway, part of you is. Don't ask me what part, I've never understood souls and everything at all. And part of me has been here since I died."

"Why?" Sorel leaned back and relaxed, letting him even out her pocketknife haircut. "Who's Agrat bat Machlat?"

"She's an angel," said Isser. "Everyone knows that."

"My father doesn't let superstitious servants stay in his house," said Sorel. "So, no, not everyone."

Isser sighed, exasperated. "Hasn't anyone ever told you not to go out alone on a Wednesday night? Or on the Eve of Shabbat?"

Sorel shrugged. Maybe. "I wouldn't have listened if they had."

"Well, those are the nights the lady goes riding with her demons," said Isser. "And if you're not careful, she'll steal you."

"So, what, you've been stolen?"

"No. It's more complicated, in my case. But she almost stole you last Shabbat, you idiot. Who goes to a bathhouse in the middle of the night no matter what day it is?"

"I was dirty!" Sorel protested.

"God protect us," said Isser. "Anyway, she got a look at you then, and now she wants to speak to you. So here you are."

The owl servant held up a towel, which Sorel took as a hint that she ought to get out of the bath and dry herself. While she wrapped herself in the one towel, the pages industriously scrubbed her limbs dry with two more. It was a far cry from her cold night in the Kuritsev bathhouse.

When she was dry, Isser helped her dress in the clothes the cat-servant had been holding: a Hussar's uniform, crusted with golden embroidery. It felt very strange to wear, but when Isser guided her to a mirror, she found that she liked what the shape of it did to her appearance—broadening her shoulders and making her chest look deep and flat. With the whisper of a mustache on her upper lip, plucked for her wedding but growing back now, and her hair cropped neatly short, she almost believed that she was a real officer.

She caught Isser's eye in the mirror and grinned at him. He gave her a crooked smile in return, as if he couldn't help it.

"You look all right," he said. "Try not to tell her any secrets, will you? Even if she likes you, she has reasons to trick you."

"The angel that steals people?"

"Yes, only don't call her that to her face. You can just say 'my lady.' She likes when people are polite."

Sorel wasn't the most practiced at politeness, but she was intrigued by the house and everything in it and couldn't help wondering about its mistress. She'd never heard of a female angel, much less one that ran with demons. Was this the sort of thing boys learned in their yeshivas? Only, no, Isser didn't have that kind of learning. Maybe it was the sort of thing people learned from their mothers.

The two little creature-servants escorted Sorel down a grand staircase, leaving Isser behind—he didn't explain, and the pages walked too quickly for Sorel to turn back without losing them.

Sorel and her father usually dined in the library, leaving the dining room at his estate for holidays, Seders and such, which Sorel always hated because her father and his male guests would talk politics and scholarship and any women brought with them would try to engage her in conversation about things she didn't understand. Kalman would only invite guests who he deemed worthy of their house, which meant women who spoke French (Sorel didn't speak it well and this embarrassed her) and talked about music and German philosophy, neither of which she knew anything about. She was supposed to be too cultured for the adventurous novels she did read, and therefore had nothing to talk about at dinner parties and had learned to hate them.

She didn't know what to expect of a dinner hosted by a lady, much less a lady who was an angel or a demon, and who drank blood, or whatever it was Isser was afraid of. When the owl-page opened the door to a brightly lit dining room, Sorel felt an involuntary shudder of social inadequacy. The feeling left her entirely as she realized not only were the guests not the sort of cultured people her father would have approved, many of them were certainly not even human. Admittedly they were all seated already and looking at her, as if they'd been expecting her arrival—but there, on the left, a young man was looking at her with a pair of cat's eyes in his otherwise ordinary head and across the table from him was the girl with the inky hair from the parade on Sabbath eve and behind them was a creature like a wolf on its hind legs, dressed in a fine silk waistcoat, and next to him was a girl with dripping wet tresses who might have been a rusalka and, then, another owl-head.

"Alter ben Kalman!" the kitten servant announced, in a yowling voice. Sorel hadn't realized the little imps could talk and jumped at the announcement.

"Our guest of honor!" cried a lovely female voice, accented with something familiar but unplaceable. It belonged to the lady at the head of the table, tall, dressed in a ruby-studded evening gown of the same last-century style as Isser's uniform, her masses of dark curls elaborately pinned atop her head. She smiled and gestured to the empty seat beside. "Baruch haba, Alter."

Sorel—Alter—stepped forward, and the guests made polite applause then returned to their meal. Some of them were eating delicacies such as Sorel-Alter could imagine seeing on any human table, but the owl-headed woman was politely carving slices off what was, unmistakably, a huge, raw mouse. Sorel-Alter shuddered and turned back to the lady—Agrat bat Machlat.

"I appreciate you accepting my invitation," Agrat said, laying her warm hand over Sorel-Alter's. "I've wanted to speak to you for some time. Did you enjoy my gift?"

"Your, uh, gift?" Sorel-Alter found it difficult to speak with the lady making eye contact. Her eyes were a deep golden color, difficult to look away from. She was really very beautiful. Sorel-Alter had not quite intended to follow Isser's advice and be cautious, but Agrat's beauty was too much. It was terrifying.

Agrat laughed, a rich, deep sound. Sorel-Alter tore their eyes away, looking instead at the glittering table setting—fork and knife of polished bone, a crystal glass of wine. Was it safe to drink wine here?

"The body in the river," the lady explained. "That was my gift to you—no one will now be looking for Sorel Kalmans. Clever, don't you think?"

Sorel-Alter's gaze was drawn inescapably back to her face. "The body? You mean—it wasn't. It wasn't real, was it?"

Agrat bat Machlat simply smiled.

Sorel-Alter caught sight of Isser standing in the shadows by the door. He caught their eye and made a face which seemed to indicate they were doing a bad job. His disapproval was, somehow, reassuring.

"Be polite" he'd said. "Thank you, my lady. That was, uh, a very—unexpected generosity."

"It was nothing," said Agrat bat Machlat. "Please. Eat."

Sorel-Alter looked to Isser again. He gave a tiny nod, and they turned to their plate. It was not a raw mouse, thankfully, but a roasted quail, appetizing in a honey glaze. When they cut into it, they found it stuffed with mushrooms and currants, sweet and dark and rich. The food filled them up like nothing they'd eaten all day in Esrog.

"Now," said Agrat bat Machlat, after awhile, "there is one little thing you might help me with, if you felt the need to show your gratitude for my assistance."

It didn't take a diplomat to understand she wasn't really asking how they felt. "What's that?" they asked, brightly and perfectly civil but meticulously worded. Making no promises.

"There is something of mine that was stolen from me," said the angel. Her plate was empty, but she traced some invisible pattern on it with a finger as she spoke. "It is somewhere in the city, but I cannot get it. I am not able to set foot in Esrog at this time."

"Why not?" said Sorel-Alter, surprised. "You seem, well. Powerful."

"Thank you, dear." Agrat patted them on the shoulder, then went back to drawing her invisible patterns. "The Esroger Rebbe is an old enemy of mine. As I understand it, you don't like him much yourself?"

"I don't know that much about him, to be honest," said Sorel-Alter, then caught Isser's eye again and shoved a forkful of quail in their mouth to stop being so honest.

"He set up his Eruv very carefully, to keep certain presences out of the city," said Agrat. "But this is not how things are meant to be. Do you understand? I have an ancient contract with rabbis much greater than that man. Certain times and places are mine, other times and places are interdict. It is unfair to me that the contract be made so strict."

It was a surprisingly petty complaint. After all, what was Esrog? Just a city. On the other hand, Sorel-Alter understood the aggravation of being told by a man where they could and could not go.

"And what is it that's in the city?" they asked.

"A book," said Agrat simply. "Just a little book. It's not so special to look at—old. But it is important to me."

"Not the book—Sefer—the Book of the Angel of Silence?"

"I had asked another to retrieve it for me," said Agrat bat Machlat. "But he failed." She gestured to Isser, still half-visible against the wall in his servant's uniform. "And now he owes me a great debt. His debt cannot be repaid without that book. And now that you and he are the same—neither can yours."

Her smile was different this time. More teeth in it. Sorel-Alter smiled back, uneasy.

"Do you know who has it?" they asked, though it felt risky to push. "The person who killed Isser?"

"It happened in the city," said Agrat. This seemed to be a no. "Do you know?"

Sorel-Alter was running through what they knew about Isser's death again. If it happened in the city, it truly couldn't be Shulem-Yontif, could it? He and Isser met on the other side of the river, in the same cemetery where Sorel-Alter was sleeping now, or had left Sam and Adela sleeping, however this worked. It could have been Pavlikov, but if so, it seemed unlikely to be connected to the book. What would a gentile know about a Jewish holy book?

They didn't want to consider the rebbe as a possibility. He was too close to their father. Yoshke, then, maybe.

"No," they said at last. "I don't know."

"Isser does not remember," said Agrat. "It torments him. You will have to find out for all our sakes. Now, before you go, my dear . . . there's one more thing you ought to know. You've been trusting someone you shouldn't."

Sorel-Alter blinked. "Who? Not Adela? Surely?"

"No, no. Adela, what a lovely girl she is. No. When you wake up, Alter, take a look in Sam's bag. Remember that, all right? Now. Drink your wine."

CHAPTER 18

Sorel woke to the glare of the moon high overhead. Adela was sound asleep next to her, curled up with her head under her blanket, but the space where Sam had been lying was empty. His blanket was still laid out on the ground, the peddler's pack he'd been using as a pillow at its head, giving the eerie impression that he'd only just left.

"Check his bag" Agrat bat Machlat had said. For what?

Sorel stood up and glanced around, checking the shadows between the gravestones for any sign of him, but saw no movement. She crawled to the pack and opened it up. The bag he kept food in was on top—she put a piece of bread in her mouth as she moved it aside. Underneath that was a spare shirt with an unwashed, animal smell, as if he'd been sleeping in a lot of barns. She put that aside with a grimace.

The next thing her hand found was the dagger. Something about its weight warned her of danger even before she drew it out and found herself holding a curved blade like an eagle's claw, sheathed in silver inlaid with black. It was ice-cold and nearly as long as her forearm, and when she slid it out of the sheath, it caught the moonlight and almost seemed to glow.

It was heavy, sharp, and expensive.

It did not look like something that belonged to a boy who slept in stables and study halls.

Sorel, barely breathing, slid the blade back into its sheath and tucked it into her vest. Reaching into the pack again, she felt the crinkle of paper. Pamphlets: a story by Ayzik Meyer Dik, a booklet of psalms, Hebrew words she didn't recognize that looked like they were amulets. And a note in a stiff Yiddish handwriting she recognized when she held it up to the moonlight. A brief note: *Find Israel. Bring him to me, or bring me the book. K.S.*

Kalman Senderovich.

Her father.

Sam was working for her father.

And her father knew about the book.

She stuffed the papers hastily back into the pack and went to shake Adela by the shoulder. "Adela! Wake up. We have to go."

"What is it?" Adela sat up, groggy. "It's dark."

"I think Sam is working for someone," Sorel hissed. "I don't trust him. We need to go to Kalman's estate."

Adela was already pulling her boots on. "Where is he?"

"I don't know, but I don't want to be here if he comes back with those city guards, or whoever it is." She was trying to remember all the men's faces, check them against people she'd seen doing work for her father, but it was no good. Certainly her father had worked with city guards. He was a leader of the Jewish community. She felt foolish for ignoring what had been right in front of her face.

They stuffed their blankets into their bag and climbed the cemetery wall into the woods. Sorel thought she knew the directions and set out into the trees with confidence. If they just followed the road, while staying off it, they'd get to her father's house. Adela didn't question the direction, keeping silent until they were well away from the cemetery.

"Why are we going to Kalman's estate?" she asked, after a while.

"I think he knows something after all. I'm sorry for doubting you before. It just seemed . . ." she trailed off. She didn't quite know how to put it. "I just thought if Isser was involved with so many criminals, why would it be someone who spends his whole life upholding the law?"

Adela snorted. "Alter, what do you think a criminal is, exactly? Are you imagining only Yoshke and Pavlikov? Kalman Senderovich doesn't uphold the law." She said it in Russian, for emphasis. "He's been one of Isser's best customers for books that aren't approved by the censors."

"What, really?"

"Everyone only follows the law when it's convenient," said Adela. "And that applies to no one more than a man who can get away with it."

Sorel chewed over this as they picked their way between the trees, keeping the moon behind them. She wondered if any of her own books—the ones her father gave her so that she'd have a European, sophisticated education—had been smuggled through Isser's hands.

She rubbed her thumb over the amulet Sam had given her, the one that was supposed to let her talk to a ghost. She had talked to him, hadn't she? She'd gone to Agrat's mansion.

Did we know each other? she asked him silently. *Did you pick me for a reason?*

It took awhile, as if he'd had to wake from a deep sleep, but she felt him stirring, felt the strange doubling in her vision as he blinked himself awake behind her eyes.

Did my father do this to you? she asked. *Is this some kind of revenge?*

Is what some kind of revenge? said Isser. *Where are we? What are you doing?*

"We're going to Kalman's estate," she said, under her breath but aloud, so Adela could hear. "We're going to see if he's got that book you were killed for, and if he does have it, we're going to—we're going to find out where your body is."

Adela looked around, eyes wide. "What did you say?"

"I'm talking to Isser," said Sorel. "Where have you been, by the way? I've been trying to talk to you, and there wasn't even a whisper of you all day, and then you're in a demon's house, acting cryptic?"

It was less disconcerting when Isser spoke this time than it had been the first time, during the card game. "Hi, Adela."

Sorel was about to protest this non-answer when Adela turned and threw her arms around them. She was warm, her arms firmly muscular, her hair soft against Sorel's neck. Isser wrapped their arms around her in return, and for a minute they just stood, holding each other, Sorel feeling like an alien in her own skin.

"I'm sorry," Isser whispered.

"You should have told me," said Adela. "You knew you were in danger; you should have told me."

"I didn't want to get you in trouble."

"So you put yourself in trouble? Alone? Stupid!" She pulled out of the hug, pinched their cheek, and turned away, wrapping her arms around herself and starting to walk again in the direction they'd been heading. Sorel felt suddenly very cold and lonely. "What's this about demons?"

"Agrat bat Machlat," said Isser. "It's her book we're looking for. She's the Angel of Death from the title. And I didn't want to say too much in her house, because if we do find it, we're not giving it back to her. And I don't want her to know that, because she'll kill us."

"Why?" Sorel asked. "What does it say?"

Adela glanced back at them and made a face. "It's very creepy when you change like that."

"I don't like it either," they said together, and Isser went on, "It's a contract with the rebbe, or with his ancestors anyway. It's an agreement that she'll guard the city from certain types of disasters and never step foot within it, but it's also . . . I don't know, it's not only disasters. It's more complicated than that. She says she's an angel of changes. And I don't think she's lying about that, because Kalman Senderovich thought so, too."

"Changes?" Adela repeated.

"Right. Like how a dead thing changes into fertile earth, I guess."

"So Kalman," said Sorel. "He does know about the book. You could have told me."

I thought you'd be angry, said Isser silently.

"Well, I am angry!" She stamped her foot at him, and then felt singularly ridiculous when Adela glanced at them again. "What, did you think I'd run to him and turn you in? Turn myself in?"

If I thought that, I wouldn't have come to you in the first place. His inner voice was sullen, and she could tell he didn't like that Adela was watching them argue. *I came to you because you were the right person. It's not revenge. You were ready to run and you just didn't know it.*

Adela raised her eyebrows. Sorel deliberately looked the other way, holding up a hand for her to wait. "Did he kill you? Tell me. Did he kill you?"

I don't know, I don't know. His anguish flooded through her, her anger crumbling underneath it. *I don't want it to be him. But I lied to him, and he wouldn't have liked it.*

"Alter," said Adela, reaching out and taking Sorel's hand. "I need to ask you something."

"What?" Sorel said, and was startled to find her voice was choked with tears. They were both crying—Sorel and Isser. Adela pulled them to a halt and made them sit on the cold ground, crouching beside them.

"Who are you?" she asked. "How do you know the way to Kalman's estate?"

It was not the question Sorel had expected.

Adela squeezed their hand, harder. "I'm trusting you because of Isser. But I need to know what you're hiding. Before we go any further."

Sorel remembered the corpse's face—her own drowned face—looking back at her. Agrat bat Machlat had provided the perfect cover for her escape. Would she give that up now? She didn't want to. She didn't want to go back.

But this was Adela. Did she really think Adela would share the secret?

The girl's eyes were dark, intense, and unwavering. Her hand was strong, her grip just shy of too tight. She was following Sorel through the forest in the middle of the night, on their way to look for murder evidence.

"The truth," said Sorel. "The truth is I'm—I was—I don't know. I am or was Kalman's daughter."

Adela blinked. "The one who died?"

"It's a trick. She had my face. The body in the mikveh. My own face! But it's almost . . ."

She was about to say something incredible. Something she almost didn't believe.

Isser nudged her, encouraging.

"It's almost better," Sorel said. "To think that no one will ever, ever guess that I'm still here."

Adela was frowning, puzzled. "You're Soreh bas Kalman?"

"I was. I don't know if I still am. I don't want to be."

Adela relaxed her grip, sitting back on her haunches. She looked over Sorel's face, a long, quiet inspection. Sorel wiped Isser's tears from their face.

"I don't want my father to be a murderer," she said. "But I'm afraid that he is. And if he is, I have to know."

CHAPTER
19

THEY REACHED KALMAN'S estate before dawn, Sorel limping on her tired feet. She meant to sneak into the house by the window in her father's study, which faced the forest. Any servants working in the kitchen or stables wouldn't be disturbed—she hoped—and Kalman himself should be asleep.

The house was dark. On the other hand, when they crept up to the back gate and Sorel boosted Adela up to look over the wall, Adela reported that there were a few carriages in the yard.

"Guests for my shiva," said Sorel, feeling strangely giddy. Adela's weight on her shoulder made her feel not burdened, but stronger in a way that would have been embarrassing to share with Isser, except he felt it too.

"Will it be a problem?" Adela asked. "I count three of them. I think one might be the rebbe."

"I don't think so. My father's study isn't in the same part of the house as the guests. He likes his quiet, though. He'll be asleep on the floor above, so we will have to be careful. The rebbe sleeps like a rock. I've heard the servants complaining about it when he's been here before."

"And Shulem-Yontif?" Adela asked, dropping to the ground and shaking out her skirts. She'd tucked them into her belt, so they hung only to her knees, still wearing Isser's trousers underneath.

Sorel hesitated. She didn't know anything about Shulem-Yontif. She'd never bothered to be interested.

"He's fine," said Isser. "If he wakes up and finds us, all we have to do is explain. He'll do what you say."

"You know, some people would say that's not the sort of husband you have to run away from," Adela teased, jostling Sorel with her elbow.

"It wasn't *just* him," Sorel protested. "I told you, didn't I? It was everything."

"I'm teasing. I'd have done the same."

Adela was to stand lookout while Sorel climbed into the study and searched for the book. She would know, more or less, what was out of place in Kalman's study. Isser would know if there was anything that belonged to him.

With Adela, they'd agreed that if they found the book they would take it and run. Isser said he thought it was dangerous for it to be outside of the city, so they'd take it back there. Sorel envisioned, romantically, stealing a horse and riding it back along the moonlit road, but she knew they'd just be back in the forest walking through the mud.

Between them, secretly, she and Isser had agreed that they weren't sure they would run. If they found a sign that Kalman was a murderer, neither of them could simply let that go. But Adela would tell them it was dangerous and stupid to do anything but retreat and regroup, so they hadn't told her.

Kalman's study had glass windows, with wooden shutters over them. The shutters were closed and locked, of course, but Sorel twisted Sam's eagle-claw dagger behind the lock and snapped it off. Adela caught it before it could hit the ground and tucked it into her pocket. The glass windows were lead-framed, opening inward opposite of the shutters. There was a little latch on the inside, but it was set in soft lead that bent like putty when Sorel jammed the narrow tip of the eagle claw between the frames, and the window swung open with the smallest squeak of hinges, barely louder than a breath.

"Here," Sorel whispered. She took the other knife from her pocket and offered it to Adela. "Take this, just in case."

Adela nodded, her face set, and turned her back to watch the path and the riverbank. Sorel hoisted herself through the window and drew the shutters closed, locking herself and Isser away in the dark. She knew this room, but only by lamplight— she hadn't exactly practiced sneaking around her father's rooms at night. But there was a soft glow in the bottom of the fireplace, and there would be candles on the mantle. She crept across the rug, avoiding her father's monumental desk by touch, and felt for the box of candles, barely breathing. There was a strange fear creeping up her back, the same feeling that had made her jump from her own window on the night of her wedding. Isser's fear, she realized now.

"You really think he could have done it?" she whispered. Her fingers closed on a candlestick, and she lifted it from the box with care, as if the slightest jostling noise could have woken Kalman on the floor above.

I don't know, said Isser. *I told him I was getting him the book, but I didn't want to give it to him. I don't remember what happened on the day I died. The last thing I know is I was going to meet his messenger at my shul, the Papermakers'. It was what we usually did. An easy place to find me. I wanted to talk to him, your father. I wanted him to explain what he needed the book for, and then . . . I don't know. I was hoping he'd say something I could agree with.*

But he didn't think Kalman would. He'd been expecting an answer he wouldn't like.

"What would you have done if he said something else?" Sorel asked, crouching to touch the candlewick to the glow in the embers. It flared to life so suddenly that she almost dropped it, blinking away spots as Isser steadied her hand.

I can't remember, said Isser. *I think maybe I would have done something stupid.*

Right. "Me too, I suppose. Like jump out a window, no?"

There was a lamp sitting at the other end of the mantle from the candle box. Sorel glanced around the room first, to dispel the creeping feeling that someone was behind her, then set the candle into the lamp so the wax wouldn't drip on her hands. Kalman's desk loomed in front of them like some great, crouching beast. She didn't want to step closer to it—as if the light might show it to be covered in blood, or she might open a drawer and find Isser's body, tucked away among the ledgers.

There was nothing on top of the desk but an inkwell, a pen set neatly beside it. Kalman was precise, organized. He wouldn't leave a secret lying in plain view. Sorel laid the lamp on the floor, kneeling to open the drawers. They were locked, but when Sorel pried at the panels with the eagle-claw dagger, the locks snapped out of place. Her father would know at once that there had been an intruder, but Isser's panic was infecting her, and she no longer cared about anything but finding answers as quickly as possible.

There were no blood-soaked daggers or gruesome trophies. The first drawer was packed neatly with pocket notebooks, each labeled on the spine with a date: Kalman's personal records. The next held a much heavier ledger, labeled as records of the Jewish community. Sorel checked underneath and behind it and found nothing but a few specks of dust.

The last drawer wasn't papers at all. There was a box and inside it were a few pieces of jewelry: Sorel's mother's rings, her headpiece decorated with pearls, and a few pairs of earrings. Sorel would have worn the headpiece if she'd married Shulem-Yontif. She held it for a moment, trying to imagine the person she would have been with pearls on her forehead. Her hands were dirty, already forming callouses from all the things she'd done in the last few days, her nail beds cracked. They didn't look like a young bride's hands.

She put the headpiece back in the box. She would not be that person again. Not for anyone.

As she closed the lid of the jewelry box, her hand brushed something soft, hidden in the very back of the drawer, in the shadows. When she drew it out, she knew that it didn't belong there. She knew because her hands were suddenly not hers, because it was Isser who was looking out behind their eyes, who recognized what they were looking at, who knew every stitch of what they were holding.

A tfillin case, embroidered with a pair of foxes.

CHAPTER
20

ISSER DIDN'T WEAR his father's tfillin. He hadn't even kept
them. They were in a trunk in Adela's room, in the Pinskers'
attic, with everything else that had belonged to Isser's parents.
Safe, and half-forgotten.

He unbuttoned the embroidered case and spilled its contents
onto the floor with shaking hands. The counterfeit censor's
stamp hit the carpet with a thump and Sorel picked it up,
turning it over to inspect it. She'd never seen one before, but
she knew the shape of it. This was the stamp that made her
father's political books look legitimate, if you didn't know
what you were seeing. It had never occurred to her that the
stamp might be a fraud.

The other thing in the bag was a pamphlet, on cheap rag
paper bound with three stitches. The strong medicinal scent of

it made them sneeze. Sorel flipped this over too, eyes skipping over the lines of Hebrew that neither of them understood.

Sefer Dumah.

A dog barked outside, deep and loud, and suddenly the shutters were thrown open. Adela leapt through the window, landing awkwardly. The lamp flickered in the sudden breeze.

"What is it?" Sorel-Isser stuffed the pamphlet back in the tfillin case, rolling it up and tucking it into their coat pocket. Adela had fallen to the floor and the shutters were clattering as something outside scrabbled against them, something heavy and ungainly trying to get in by throwing its weight against the heavy wood. Sorel-Isser ran to shut the windows, trying to twist the broken latch back into place, but it was useless. A deep, low growl sounded from outside.

"A dog," said Adela, breathless. "Your father has a guard dog?"

"No, he doesn't." They grabbed her hand and hauled her to her feet, backing toward the door as the dog slammed itself against the shutters again and again. How long would it take for the dog to stop and try another way? The shutters weren't locked. It was pure luck that Adela had managed to slam them closed behind her. If the dog wedged its snout under the edge, it could open them. "I would have told you if he had a guard dog. He does *not* have a dog."

Their heel hit the door. They felt for the handle without taking their eyes off the window, pushed it open, and fled into the hallway, slamming the door behind them. There was no lock, but there was a cabinet in the hallway, a heavy, polished piece with a candelabra on it, its only purpose to show off Kalman's wealth and good taste. Sorel-Isser grabbed one end of it and Adela grabbed the other, dragging it across to block the door just as they heard shattering glass inside the study.

"What the hell is that?" Adela gasped. They could hear it panting, sniffing around the room as if it were searching for something. The quiet scratching of its claws was worse than the thundering bark. The rest of the house was silent as a grave. Surely the barking would have woken someone. The servants, Kalman, the guests.

"I don't know," said Sorel-Isser, grabbing her hand again. They ran for the kitchens, to the door that would take them to the stable-yard and out of the house and as far from the dog as possible. "It's been following me for days. It killed—"

They stopped as someone stepped out of the kitchen, blocking the hallway in front of them. They'd left the lamp in the study, and the only windows were at the end of the hallway behind them, so the light pouring in from the kitchen blinded them for a moment. A silhouette stood before them. But they didn't have to see his face to know it was him. They didn't even have to think.

He was holding a lantern in his hand, which he lifted to their faces as they stood frozen in their tracks, blinking in the glare of the light. His face was dazed, as if he'd just woken from a deep sleep, and there were bags under his eyes.

"Israel?" he said, in a tone of confusion, then leaned closer, blinking as if he too had been blinded. He lifted his empty hand to their face, tucked his fingers under their chin, and turned their head from side to side, scrutinizing every angle of their features as if it were a difficult holy text, written without vowels. "Soreh?"

"Papa," Sorel breathed, and then Isser said, "You *killed* me."

"No," said Kalman. He took a step back, looking suddenly very old and fragile. Sorel realized they were the same height. She had always thought that he was taller. But she'd never really looked him in the eye before. "No. Who are you?"

Sorel-Isser took the tfillin case from their pocket and held it up to him. "Where did you get this? This is *mine*. His. You had those men search my room."

"Yes," said Kalman. He took their wrist, in a strangely gentle grip, and pulled them toward the kitchen door. They followed, dragging Adela behind them. She shut the door and stood against it, holding the latch and listening for movement in the hallway.

In the better light of the kitchen, Kalman set his lantern on the table and looked them over again, with that same searching look. "It *is* you. Both of you. Sarah, and Israel— but one of you is dead, and the other—I've been looking for you."

"Looking for me?"

"Ostap said you'd run. Disappeared. I sent messengers to the shtetlach, trying to find you and the book, and nothing. I always knew you were clever. I thought I was more so."

"What do you mean, looking for the book," Sorel protested. "It's here, you have it."

"Take a better look," said Kalman, with a bitter twist of a smile. "You outfoxed me, Israel. Rebound it, hm? All that work to convince you, and you were never planning to hand it over."

Sorel-Isser dropped Adela's hand to take the pamphlet from the bag and look it over again, turning the pages. The outer pages were right, printed in cramped Hebrew. But the inner pages—Sorel recognized the text. It was a women's prayer book, in Yiddish. "But then, where's the real one?"

Adela peered over their shoulder.

"I sent Ostap to find you," said Kalman. "To get it. He came back with nothing. We searched your rooms, and again—nothing. Not a sign of you. And no one in Kuritsev had seen you come through to tell Adela where you'd gone."

"I've been here the whole time," said Isser. "I never left. Don't lie to me! You knew where I would be—the Papermakers' Shul. You knew I'd have the book. And you didn't want anyone to know that I'd taken it for you, so why *wouldn't* you kill me? I'm not your Kaddish. I'm a tool to you." They threw the pamphlet to the floor and stepped forward. "So what did you do with my body?"

"Isser," said Adela cautiously, reaching for their hand again.

"How can you keep looking me in the face and lying?" Sorel-Isser demanded. Kalman Senderovich, in his dressing gown, no longer looked untouchable. Their hands were shaking, but it wasn't fear anymore. Now it was anger. They wanted to grab him, shake him, throw him off his feet. They wanted to sink their teeth into him. "How could you do *any* of it? Destroy the city's protection, just because it's out of your control. Make me steal from the rebbe, make me *marry his son* while you're lying to him, calling him your friend while you're trying to destroy him. What's wrong with you?"

"That is not what happened," Kalman breathed. He had not stepped away. But he didn't draw himself up. He stood half-slumped, leaning lightly on the edge of the table. "I did everything for you. Everything. So that you would have a better life."

"You didn't do it for *me*." Sorel-Isser spat. "You did it for yourself. For your legacy."

"Isser," said Adela. "Alter! Listen."

They all stopped for a moment, holding their breaths. The house was still quiet, as if it were only the three of them. Not a sound from the bedrooms upstairs or the servants' closet just off the kitchen, where the cook should have been waking from her sleep.

And in the hallway, the quiet scuffing of a large dog's claws on the floorboards.

"How did it get out?" Adela whispered, and then the latch on the kitchen door rattled. They all stood, staring at the door. It was not the scratching of a dog on the other side anymore, but the frantic maneuvering of someone with hands. The latch clicked open, and they all backed away from the door.

The dog was gone.

The person standing in the hallway, barefoot and in his shirtsleeves, was Sam.

CHAPTER

21

SAM SHOOK OUT HIS HANDS, as if he'd just washed them, and stepped over the threshold. His fingers ended in thick black claws, long as a bear's.

"Isser Jacobs," he said. "I want my knife back and I want the book. I know it's here—I can smell it."

Sorel-Isser had forgotten the knife. It was tucked into their belt. Remembering, they pulled it from the sheath. Before they could make another move, Adela picked up the pamphlet from the floor and tossed it to Sam.

"We don't have your book," she said. "That's a fake."

Rather than open it to check the pages, as the others had done, he held it up and shook it. Then he held it to his nose and sniffed, frowning. Though he looked the same as always, he held himself differently, as if at any moment he might leap forward. Sorel-Isser gripped the handle of the eagle-claw knife more tightly as Sam opened the book at last and read one of the psalms.

"Clever," he said, an echo of Kalman earlier, and tucked the pamphlet away in his back pocket. When he turned his gaze on them, Sorel-Isser saw what was strange about his face— he still had the dark, white-less eyes of the great black dog. "Where is it, then?"

Sorel-Isser met his eyes and stood their ground. "Who are you?"

Adela glanced between them, confused. "He's not the angel?"

"Not *that* angel," said Sam. "There were three parties to the bargain with the first Esroger Rebbe—the rebbe, Dumiel, and Kaftziel. Dumiel is my sister, the demon Agrat. And I am the other Angel of Death. My sister's been hiding you, Isserke, hasn't she? You're going to take the book to her, and she'll grant you a wish, is it? I can't let you do that."

"We don't have it," Sorel-Isser repeated, glancing around at Kalman. "I hid it before I talked to Kalman Senderovich, but I don't remember where. I don't remember anything from the day I died. Was it *you* that killed me?"

"Me?" Sam looked almost offended. "Why would I do that? You were no business of mine until you were dead already."

"But you're working together." Sorel-Isser pointed to Sam and Kalman with the knife, one after the other. "I found the note in your bag. You're one of his messengers."

Sam shook his head. Kalman said, "I don't know him. He isn't working for me."

"I found that note with one of the men I killed for you in Esrog," said Sam. "One of those city uniformed gentiles. What was he called?" He glanced at the ceiling, as if he could see the name written there. "Borysko."

"There's a Borysko in the city guard," said Kalman. Sam's arrival had seemed to drain him of all remaining energy, and he now sat slumped against the kitchen table. "A young man. He collects the taxes sometimes. He takes bribes. Ostap introduced me to him. Please, Sarah and Israel. Believe that I wanted the best for you. I won't stop you now. Whatever you want to do—just do it."

"Wait," said Adela. She was reaching out a hand to Sorel-Isser, and another to Sam, though neither had made any move. "Wait. No one do anything. Everyone wants the book—fine. Everyone is willing to kill to get it or die to protect it. Before you do that, let's talk."

"I wasn't planning to kill anyone," said Sam. "Isserke's already dead. He's mine already. He has no right to keep hiding. That body belongs to Alter."

"Alter doesn't mind sharing," said Sorel. "And you said you don't want Agrat to have the book, didn't you? Well, we're not planning to hand it over to her, either. Isn't that right? Right. She wants to break the rebbe's protection. Isser didn't trust her. I don't trust her, either. She was too nice to me."

Sam glanced at Kalman, but the older man had put his head in his hands, almost as if he were praying. He seemed to have made his last contribution to the discussion.

"All right," said Sam reluctantly. "Then we agree. You can give back my knife."

"We're not giving you anything if you're planning to steal Isser's soul," said Adela.

Sam threw up his hands in a gesture of exasperation that was all human, an echo of the cheerful peddler. Was it a disguise? Or just another facet of the same person? "It isn't stealing! It belongs to me. But fine, I've waited this long. You can stay until your business is concluded, how's that for a bargain?"

Sorel didn't want to mistrust him. After all, he *had* been helping. He'd run off the men who wanted to kill her and Isser, the first day in Esrog. Although he could have done it in a less terrifying manner.

"A bargain," she agreed. "But I'll keep this knife, for now. You can help us, and we'll help you. But if you're planning some kind of trick, we won't give it back, and you can see which of us finds the book faster."

Sam spat in his palm and held it out to them. When they hesitated, eyeing the long claws, he took his hand back, wiped it on his trousers, and offered it again—this time, a soft, human hand, with nails bitten short.

Sorel-Isser took it, and Adela clasped her hand over theirs.

"Now we have to talk to Ostap," said Isser.

THEY LEFT KALMAN in the kitchen, already succumbing again to the spell of sleep that Sam had cast over the rest of the household, even the shiva guests. Ostap—Sorel had never paid him much attention, but this was the gentile stable-boy whose coat she was wearing. He slept in the tack room.

When they arrived, he was wide awake, dressed and standing in the stable doors with a hunting rifle over his shoulder, glancing around like a guardsman on patrol, but too afraid to enter the house from where he'd heard the barking of the giant dog.

Ostap had not slept, in fact, in days. He had been waiting for word from his brother, Borysko, to say that all was well in the city, and Borysko had found the magic book which Isser, that bastard, had stolen from Reb Kalman.

Word from Borysko had never come, and in his dreams Ostap was hunted by a great black dog. Its presence seemed to follow him into the waking world, watching from over his shoulder, but always disappearing when he turned his head.

The conclusion the stable-boy had reached was that Isser Jacobs was a witch, and that by turning him over to the city guard, Ostap had called down a curse on his own head. Now the dog had come to Reb Kalman's estate, and he was sure it had eaten Reb Kalman. He'd seen a light in the old man's window, and then the light had gone out, and the barking had stopped.

Ostap was waiting to die.

This was how Sorel-Isser and Adela found him when they went out into the courtyard, where the rising sun was just beginning to burn away the mist from the river. He cocked the rifle at them, but he had not expected death to come wearing his own clothes. That was what stopped him, for a second, from firing. And in that moment, he saw Isser, looking out from behind Sorel's face.

"How are you back?" he demanded. "Borysko said he was sure he'd killed you! All this time I've been shitting myself, thinking Reb Kalman would find out that it was my fault, and you're not even dead?"

"Borysko's dead," said Sorel-Isser. Adela grabbed their arm, as if to drag them out of the way. Ostap took a step back, his arm shaking. If he fired the gun, the shot would go wild.

"You killed him?"

Isser stepped forward. Sorel could have stopped him, but there was something exhilarating about ignoring their fear, pretending to be the monster Ostap thought they were. As if by simply ignoring the possibility of a bullet, they could make themselves bulletproof. "What did you do with my body, Ostap? Where did you leave me?"

"Stop! Don't come any closer. I didn't kill you. It was Borysko. I didn't tell him to kill you! I didn't think he was going to kill you." The tip of the rifle dipped, and he corrected it. "Reb Kalman said to bring you back. I told Borysko. I said, we have to find out where you've hidden that magic book. Reb Kalman would have made us rich. I'd never have to shovel another load of manure, not ever. I'd get the good jobs. Like the jobs you'd always get, you ungrateful dog! All that Reb Kalman's done for you, and you turn around and bring your bastard witchcraft into his house. He's a good Jew, Reb Kalman. He keeps his promises. But you wouldn't *talk*. I told you Borysko knew you'd been smuggling; I told you I saw you with that old witch in the Jews' graveyard. I know all your secrets! Everything you've done. What's one more secret, to save your life?"

He was shouting, scarcely seeing them in front of his face. Sorel-Isser stumbled back as a sudden pain stabbed them under their ribs, a memory of Ostap's horrified face. Borysko, his older brother, holding Ostap's knife, shoving Isser to the ground, and Ostap screaming.

"Where's the book?" Sorel-Isser gasped. "Just tell me where it is, and you're forgiven. I don't want to kill you."

"I don't know where it is," said Ostap. He shut his eyes for a moment, took a deep breath. Steadied his hand. "And if I did, I wouldn't tell you. You killed Borysko? Then go to hell."

Adela yanked Sorel-Isser to the side just as Ostap pulled the trigger. The black dog leapt over their heads, slamming into the stable-boy and knocking him backward to the ground. They hit one of the horse stalls with a crash, breaking through the planks and sending all the horses to screaming. The gun fired again, wild, as it spun out of Ostap's hand. Adela leapt forward before Sorel-Isser could get to their feet, grabbed the gun, and retreated. Sam had Ostap by the collar and was shaking him like a rat.

"Stop it," said Sorel-Isser. "You're going to kill him."

Sam dropped the boy in a heap and pressed one giant paw down on his chest. Ostap, covering his head with his arms, laid still and didn't try to move. Sam growled, low, the sound seeming to fill the whole world. Even Sorel-Isser felt the urge to run from it.

"Where did you leave my body?" they asked again. "This is the last chance you get. Show us, or we'll let him tear your throat out."

THEY HAD NOT BEEN FAR from Isser's body all along. A wrong turn in the forest, and Sorel could have stumbled on it, in her panicked flight from her wedding or on her way back to Kalman's estate with Adela. Ostap led them along a woodcutters' trail that cut due north from Kalman's toward Esrog, a shortcut to the Jewish Quarter and the taverns on the western side of the river along the smugglers' road. The route that Isser took to visit Kalman's estate in secret, without anyone knowing when he went in or out of the city. A route Sorel could have taken, had she known about it, and gotten to Esrog twice as quickly.

Just off the track, not far south of the river, there was a big old tree, straddling a rocky outcrop so that its roots created a hollow space. And here, when Ostap dragged aside a hasty screen of branches, was Isser's grave.

They had not really buried him. Panicked, Ostap had run from the scene, and his brother had chased him down to retrieve him. They'd come back half-hoping Isser would still be breathing, but he wasn't. He'd stared at them in accusation, with his blank dead eyes, until Ostap pulled his cap down over his face to hide it.

He was tucked into the hollow, curled up, almost like he was sleeping. But they didn't have to look closely to know that he wasn't. One of his limp hands was visible, discolored and swollen, and the smell of old blood hung in the air as heavy as a wet wool blanket.

Sorel-Isser stood staring at the hand for a long moment, then turned away to be sick in the brambles. Ostap stood hollow-eyed and frozen. Adela, braver, crept forward, one sleeve over her nose and mouth, to take a closer look.

"We have to move him," she said, voice shaking. "If we're going to—to search his pockets. Or anything. We have to move him."

"We'll have to move him to bury him," said Sam.

"He didn't have it," said Ostap. "Borysko checked. He said it must be back in the city. Hid it in his room, or something. But when Reb Kalman sent people to look there, it wasn't. And we couldn't tell him we'd found Isser and killed him. He'd have turned us in, had us hanged. He couldn't know. I'm sorry," he added, in a tone of desperation. "By God, I never meant it to happen. Why did you have to be *stubborn*?"

Sorel-Isser wiped their mouth and tried to swallow. Sorel said, *We've already seen our own dead face one time. How bad can it be?*

But neither of them believed it.

"Ach, let me do it," said Sam, at last. "Shut your eyes, kinderlech."

None of them wanted to look. Adela took Sorel-Isser's hand and leaned on their shoulder. Ostap slumped against a tree, staring into the distance like a man condemned. And Sam searched Isser's pockets.

All he came up with was a scrap of paper with a note in Yiddish. Ostap and Borysko hadn't bothered with it because they couldn't read it and they'd been in a hurry. It didn't say much anyway. Just: *Adela. Talk to Old Rukhele.*

"Rukhele the klogerin," said Sorel-Isser, when Sam read it aloud. "She's the one who told me what the book is. She lives in the river bottom and begs around the Gravediggers' Shul. I buy her a hot meal, sometimes."

"The old witch," grumbled Ostap.

CHAPTER
22

THEY WRAPPED THE BODY in Sorel-Isser and Adela's blankets and carried him with them to the river, taking turns. Ostap knew where a smuggler's boat was hidden—smugglers his brother took bribes from. They took the boat across to the Jewish Quarter, near Yoshke's boat shed. Yoshke was not at home, and they left the body there with Ostap as a reluctant guardian while Sorel-Isser, Adela, and Sam made their way to the Gravediggers' Shul to see if Old Rukhele could be found there. Sorel could feel Isser's soul curled up next to hers in bruised and grieving silence. She wanted to say something to him, but there was nothing that would make it better.

Kalman had not intended for him to die, but he had. Her father—their father. It was a thing that could not be changed. There would be no putting soul and body back together. They kept seeing the hand, his softly curled fingers, pale and discolored, cold as ice. His body was already changing, dust to dust.

It was a relief that he was still there at all, that finding the body hadn't torn them apart. But only barely.

Adela jostled them with her shoulder, drawing them out of their reverie, and laced her fingers through theirs. Her hand was warm, almost hot, and her grip reassuringly heavy. She didn't say anything, but she didn't need to.

At the Gravediggers' Shul, the men were praying the morning service. There was a samovar on the stove at the side, brewing strong tea, and next to this were huddled a couple of elderly beggars, waiting for their cup of tea with sugar and a bit of a raisin bun, which accompanied the gossip after the regular minyan. One of the beggars, to Sorel-Isser's relief, was Old Rukhele. Sorel-Isser pointed her out to Adela and the two of them approached her quietly, while Sam stood leaning in the doorway, watching the prayer service with his arms folded.

"Grandmother?" Adela murmured, with a gentle touch to Rukhele's elbow. "I wonder if you could help me with something? My name is Adela. Did Isser tell you about me?"

"Isser . . ." Rukhele thought for a moment. "Srulka from the print shop, isn't it? He told me he had a message for an Adela, if anything happened to him. It's in your usual hiding place— that's the message."

Adela frowned. "But I checked the usual hiding place. The rafters in your room," she added, to Sorel-Isser. "That would be the usual place, wouldn't it?"

"Not in my room," said Isser. "I couldn't stand having it in my room."

"Not in your room," Rukhele agreed. "Here. It's safer, in a shul. A holy place, no?"

All but the old woman glanced upward. The Gravediggers' Shul was squat and humble, with a post-and-beam roof that reminded Sorel of the hayloft in the stables.

The rafters were not so far from the women's gallery. An agile person could have climbed into them at some point while the shul was empty and tucked a small package between the beams.

"You made it difficult for yourself, didn't you," said Adela, crossing her arms and giving Sorel-Isser an exaggerated frown. "Couldn't have kept it in your own roof?"

"It stank, and it gave me nightmares," Isser hissed. "I didn't want it watching me while I slept. I felt dybbuk-ridden whenever I touched it."

Adela raised an ironic eyebrow. Isser made a face at her, and they had to look away from each other to stop a hysterical laugh from bubbling up. The men were still praying their service.

"Thank you, grandmother," Adela whispered, pressing a coin into Old Rukhele's hand. "Be healthy."

They moved away from the old woman and her companion, but before they could return to Sam in the doorway, Adela stopped Sorel-Isser with a hand on their elbow and whispered in their ear, "What do we do once we have it?"

"I meant to find someone I could ask to help me read it," Isser explained. "If I hadn't—" He waved a hand, brushing away the unsayable. "If I'd had the time. Someone who reads the Holy Language. The only person I know well is Shulem-Yontif, and well, I didn't want to ask so much of him. He'd already stolen it for me. And I was in trouble."

"I don't know that we should just tell Sam we know where it's hidden," said Adela, glancing in his direction. "I mean, if he knows where it is, what stops him from taking it and doing what he likes with it and wasting all your effort?"

Sorel-Isser bit their thumbnail, thinking. "I have an idea. We can distract him and get ourselves a religious scholar at the same time. Two birds in one net."

Pretending Rukhele hadn't told them the book was in the Gravediggers' Shul, they reconvened outside in the street.

"She knows where the book is, but we need Shulem-Yontif's help to get it," Sorel-Isser explained to Sam. "You should go back to Kalman's estate and get him. We'll meet you at the rebbe's house."

"Why am I the one going to get Shulem-Yontif?" Sam asked. "I don't even know him."

"You're not human, are you? So your feet don't hurt."

"And you can run on all fours," Adela added. "Faster that way."

"Shulem-Yontif's about fifteen years old with black hair and black eyes, and he always looks like he wants to apologize for something," said Sorel-Isser. "He's not exactly difficult to spot. He's the rebbe's son, he'll be well-dressed."

Sam looked for a moment like he wanted to argue, then the blandly cheerful look slid back over his face. It somehow felt just as dangerous as the look of suspicion, and Sorel-Isser's hand went to the knife in their belt.

But Sam just said, "All right, then. Since we have a bargain."

Adela and Sorel-Isser sat on their heels until Sam was out of sight, and the men from the minyan started to filter out of the shul. The last to go were Rukhele and the other old beggar, fortified with the last dregs of hot tea from the samovar.

Once the shul was empty, they crept back inside and up the stairs to the women's gallery. Because of Sorel's height, it was easier for them to climb into the rafters than it had been for Isser the first time. His hands remembered where to hold on and reach into the joint between two beams to pull out the book, wrapped in oilcloth and bound into the covers of the tehillim whose pages he'd given to Kalman.

They sat on the floor of the women's gallery to work out their plan.

"The problem with the story of the first Esroger Rebbe's contract is, it was *just* the rebbe," Isser explained to Sorel and Adela. "Reb Kalman is wrong about a lot of things, but he's right that we can't only do what the rebbe says. The rebbe thinks it's bad luck to get too close to gentiles, when we live right on top of each other. We can't do only what Reb Kalman wants, either. Reb Kalman wants the Jewish community to be respectable and law-abiding, but that means sweeping our real problems under the rug. And the lady—Agrat—she wants free rein within the city. But I don't trust her either."

"So what we need is a new contract," said Adela. "An agreement between the angels and the city that works for everyone. So the city can grow and change, without falling to disaster."

It was a lot to ask.

But all three of them were used to wishing the world looked different.

SAM AND SHULEM-YONTIF met them outside the rebbe's house, in the wealthier Jewish district near the Great Synagogue, though the rebbe himself rarely deigned to set foot in that Enlightened establishment. He conducted services and gave audiences to his court in his own sitting room, which was as big as a ballroom.

They left Sam outside as lookout while they pretended to look for the book hidden in the most unexpected of places—the rebbe's study, where it should have been all along. Sorel-Isser checked the box where it should have been hidden and removed the stories by Ayzik Mayer Dik while Adela explained the plan to Shulem-Yontif.

"We want to rewrite this contract with the Angels of Death, but none of us know the loshn koydesh."

Shulem-Yontif looked stricken. Adela was offering him the book, but he held up his hands, shaking his head.

"I can't read that! Papa said I mustn't. It's dangerous."

"*Not* reading it is more dangerous," said Adela. "Isser died for this. Did you know?"

This was the wrong thing to say, as it sent Shulem-Yontif into a fit of tears and handwringing over his own complicity in Isser's death, and the fact that theft was a sin, and some other incoherent troubles.

"It's fine," Sorel-Isser told him. Isser put their arm around his shoulder, over Sorel's objections. *It's not like he knows it's you, Alter.* "It wasn't your fault, Shuli. It's all right. You can make it up to him by helping us with this. You'll be a hero—Esrog's new tzadik."

"Not that anyone's going to know you're the tzadik," said Adela unhelpfully. "We're keeping all this a secret."

"A secret mitzvah is more powerful anyway," said Isser.

This argument, or either Isser's gently encouraging tone, had the desired effect, and at last Shulem-Yontif sat down in his father's chair to read over the Sefer Dumah. After a moment he laughed, lightheartedly.

"Oh, but this is simple! It's only a lot of angels' names and then very straightforward. It says the angels will protect the Jewish community of Esrog and never transgress the boundary laid out by my great-grandfather—that's the eruv, I think. They can only collect the souls of the dead *in their right time,* from the cemetery."

"And in return they get what?" Sorel asked.

"They don't really get anything," said Shulem-Yontif. "It's just that my great-grandfather was so very strong and righteous. But it must be difficult to keep an angel from breaking into the city, don't you think? No wonder Papa is so tired all the time."

"That seems a little unfair," said Adela. "I thought it would have a payment."

"It is the Angel of Death we're talking about," said Shulem-Yontif uncertainly. "He *is* evil. Or it's two angels, there's two in here—Kaftziel and Dumiel, and a lot of other names, but those are the signatories, so I think the other names are just their own names, or epithets, you know. Are you sure it wouldn't be better for Papa to explain all of this? I don't know very much about angels. Only here it says Agrat bat Machlat, also—do you know that story? Rabbi Hanina ben Dosa gave her Wednesday and Friday nights to cavort with her demons. That's why it's so unlucky to go out alone after dark. But here in this book, she's the angel Dumiel."

"She said the Esroger Rebbe stole her legal right," said Isser. "She's not allowed in the city any day at all."

"Then we have bargaining power," Adela pointed out. "We can give her back something she thinks she was supposed to have."

Except Sam also thinks there's something he's supposed to have, Sorel reminded Isser, *and that's you. But I have an idea about that.*

CHAPTER
23

THEY BROUGHT THE BOOK back to the cemetery, where Agrat bat Machlat was allowed to come and collect her souls and where Rukhele had warned Isser not to bring it, lest he summon the angel and her anger. Shulem-Yontif tagged along, reluctantly, as a representative of the Hasidim and the rebbe's bloodline, looking all the while as if he might bolt like a rabbit. To Sorel's great aggravation Isser kept giving him reassuring pats on the back or shoulder.

You're leading him on, you idiot, she told him.

He doesn't know it's me, either! And he's frightened. Be nice.

Despite Sorel's plans and the ease with which they were able to share their body now, they were not fully in agreement.

It didn't take Agrat or Dumiel long to respond to the call, simple as it was. They had been standing among the gravestones for hardly two breaths before they heard the chime of harness bells and a black horse emerged from the forest, picking its way between fallen branches with the lady on its back. Looking at her now next to Sam, Sorel-Isser could see the resemblance. They had the same bottomless eyes.

"You've brought me my book," she said sweetly. "How wonderful. You didn't have to invite Kaftziel, you know."

"My name is on the contract," said Sam. His voice was mild enough, but he'd shifted his weight a little as she approached, squaring up as if preparing to fight. "I intend to make sure you keep to your appointed boundaries, and don't get carried away spreading a plague, or flooding the river bottoms, or, God forbid, spreading libels against the Jews."

Agrat sniffed delicately and slid off her horse. She was wearing little embroidered slippers, not unlike the ones Sorel had thrown away on the night of her wedding. The angel stepped carefully between the weeds to keep her feet dry, like a cat. "The Esroger Rebbe stole my rights! Is it so unreasonable for me to want a little revenge? You'd like to take a bit of revenge, wouldn't you, Soreh bas Kalman? And you, Isser ben Yakov . . . you've been mistreated, yourself. Wouldn't you like to see them suffer, just a little? The ones who've been your enemies, who've taken power from you and given you nothing in return? Who haven't *loved* you as you have loved them?"

This last she seemed to direct to all of them, even Shulem-Yontif, who shrank back when her eyes swept over him.

"Let my brother have his righteous posturing," Agrat said, brushing her hand down Sorel-Isser's cheek. "He's powerless. You have his dagger—what can he do without it? Bark like a dog, only. He doesn't mind being constrained. He's lazy. He likes to watch and wait until the very last moment and never try to change things on his own. Not like us, no? Not like you. Let's see it, then. Let's bury it."

"We're not going to destroy the contract," said Sorel.

Agrat stepped back as if she'd been burned. "What?"

"I don't want revenge. I don't want to see anyone suffer. I just want to be free. And I understand why you want that, too. It must be boring, never getting to see what's happening in the city, shut up in your own manor house with no interesting company. But that doesn't mean you have to destroy everything. We'll give you back your Wednesday nights and your Fridays. The rebbe never should have taken those from you. But you're not allowed to take revenge on Esrog for what a rebbe did who isn't even here anymore."

The sweetness melted off Agrat's face. "I don't have to agree to your terms. I could just take that book from you now and kill you all. No one would even miss you! You're already dead."

With a low growl, Sam, dog-shaped, stepped in between them. Agrat glared at him, teeth bared, and for a moment,

Sorel-Isser thought she would leap on him and tear at him with her bare hands and teeth. But then she relaxed her shoulders, with a visible effort, and met their eyes again.

"I have been very patient," she said. "I have waited. I have kept to the terms. But time and again, I have not received what I have been promised. The Esroger Rebbe promised that if I signed that contract, Esrog would be a city of miracles and the whole world would pass by my door. Where are the miracles? No one walks this road now but beggars. I will not agree to a contract without payment."

Sam growled again, and Sorel-Isser laid a hand on his shoulder, calming. "We have an offer of payment, actually. How would you like to have the life of the princess of Esrog, Reb Kalman's daughter?"

Agrat blinked and tilted her head.

"The girl's drowned," Sorel went on. "It would be a miracle if she returned, wouldn't it? And if you were Kalman's daughter, an ordinary girl, the rebbe's contract wouldn't stop you from going anywhere at all. I'll give you everything. All of it. My place in my father's house, my name, my inheritance. You get to be human, for one lifetime. There's no better position to annoy the rebbe from. I was supposed to be his daughter-in-law, though that's not going to happen anymore. His son is running away to Odessa—there's your revenge."

"What are you doing?" Adela whispered from behind them.

"There's just one more stipulation, if you agree to that," said Sorel. "You have to let Isser stay with me. Both of you." This was directed to Sam, who'd glanced over his shoulder at them. "We're giving you everything else you want in this contract. Just let him stay."

EPILOGUE

THE SMALL GRAVEYARD on the edge of Kalman Senderovich's estate was usually choked with brambles, but it had been cleaned up to bury Sorel Kalmans. Until the girl reappeared from the forest, disoriented and chilled, claiming she'd been afflicted by a dybbuk on the night before her wedding and run in a panic, scarcely knowing where she was, surviving on forest berries and roots for days all alone. When the coffin was dug up, it was found to be empty, only a few handfuls of damp clay in the bottom, as if the drowned body had simply gotten up and walked away.

The miracle was imputed to the holiness of the Esroger Rebbe. It was, in its way, not even surprising.

The brambles were already growing back when Alter-Yisrael, Adela, and Sam brought the body that had once been

Isser to lie in the false Sorel's grave. Rumor had it that Kalman and his daughter were moving into the city itself, that the half-mad girl refused to step foot again onto the land where she'd fallen victim to the demon. Kalman Senderovich was going into the business of cutting railway ties, which was better conducted from the northwestern side of Esrog, far from the river.

Soon enough the whole estate would be eaten by the forest. No one would ever know that the empty space in the graveyard had been filled after all.

The body would lie nameless, undisturbed.

No one was looking for Alter-Yisrael or the Sefer Dumah. The book had never been missing, as far as anyone knew. On Shavuot the rebbe would look in the locked box and find the contract miraculously rewritten, but he would tell no one, just as he had told no one of the book's existence to begin with. He liked to think his own great-grandfather had returned to make the changes.

Alter-Yisrael pushed a handful of earth into the grave, then Adela, then Sam. One of Old Rukhele's crows had followed them from the river and stood on a nearby headstone, croaked "Rekh, rekh, rachamim" until Alter-Yisrael offered it a piece of a raisin bun, and it fell silent.

The scent of new growth rose out of the soil as the waning moon crept up over the trees.

THE END

ACKNOWLEDGMENTS

It's very different writing a book with the intention of writing a book than it is writing one with no plan for its future. I gave myself a hard act to follow with *When the Angels Left the Old Country*, and I hope this one lives up to expectations.

As a historical fantasy *The Forbidden Book* owes some debts to historians and fantasists of the past. I owe an obvious debt to S. An-sky and *Der Dibek*. It feels like a queer Jewish fantasist's rite of passage to do a take on the dybbuk—this is mine. The sources on women and Yiddish folklore from the website Pulling at Threads were also very useful. I took additional inspiration from Michael Stanislawski's *A Murder in Lemberg* (exploring tensions within a Jewish community of the mid-nineteenth century), S.Y. Agnon's *A City in Its Fullness*, and Alan Mintz's analysis thereof in *Ancestral Tales* (thanks to

S., who brought me a copy left over from the Association of Jewish Studies conference—a serendipitous encounter).

Thanks to my agent Rena Rossner and the team at the Deborah Harris Agency. Knowing I have experts doing my negotiations for me takes away so much stress.

Thanks and more thanks to Arthur. Your confidence in my work means so much. To Arely, Irene, Antonio, Kerry, Danielle, and the rest of the LQ team: I'm so happy to work with you all again and to be part of the wonderful lineup of LQ authors. Thanks to Will Staehle for another beautiful cover!

Thanks to all the readers whose response to *When the Angels Left the Old Country* has been so amazing, including the award committees for the Stonewall Book Award, the Sydney Taylor Book Award, the Printz Award, the Mythopoeic Award, the Jewish Book Award, the New England Book Award, and the AudioFile Earphones Award. Can you believe how long that list is?!

To everyone who's chosen *When the Angels Left the Old Country* for a book club, a class, or to give to a friend: thank you. To the librarians who have added the book to your collections and to everyone who's pushed back against library censorship in the last few years, thanks for standing up for teens' right to read.

As always, the process of moving from concept to draft to book is much easier with the support of good friends. Thanks to my Lambda cohort once again, I love you. I'm so happy to have teamed up with both Jen St. Jude and Jas Hammonds for author events and am looking forward to many more. Bird Chat and Kuzu Chat, thanks for always being there. Pip and Elise (and Glimmer and Ella and Moses)—I wrote almost this whole book on the farm, so thank you as always for hosting!

To my parents: I wouldn't be here without you. Thanks for watching Anzu when I wasn't home. And thank you, Anzu, for your little kissies. Please stop eating my earbuds. I need those.

SOME NOTES ON THIS BOOK'S PRODUCTION

The art for the jacket and case was drawn by Will Staehle using Procreate. The text was set in Cochin, originally produced in 1912 by Georges Peignot for the Paris foundry G. Peignot et Fils and based on the copperplate engravings of 18th century French artist Charles-Nicolas Cochin. It was composed by Westchester Publishing Services in Danbury, CT. The book was printed on FSC™-certified 78 gsm wood-free paper and printed and bound in China.

Production was supervised by Freesia Blizard
Book designed by Will Staehle
Interior Design by Patrick Collins
Assistant Managing Editor: Danielle Maldonado
Edited by Arthur A. Levine

LEVINE QUERIDO